# CLAUDIA AND THE LITTLE LIAR

**Other books by
Ann M. Martin**

*P.S. Longer Letter Later*
(written with Paula Danziger)
*Leo the Magnificat*
*Rachel Parker, Kindergarten Show-off*
*Eleven Kids, One Summer*
*Ma and Pa Dracula*
*Yours Turly, Shirley*
*Ten Kids, No Pets*
*Slam Book*
*Just a Summer Romance*
*Missing Since Monday*
*With You and Without You*
*Me and Katie (the Pest)*
*Stage Fright*
*Inside Out*
*Bummer Summer*

THE KIDS IN MS. COLMAN'S CLASS series
BABY-SITTERS LITTLE SISTER series
THE BABY-SITTERS CLUB mysteries
THE BABY-SITTERS CLUB series
CALIFORNIA DIARIES series

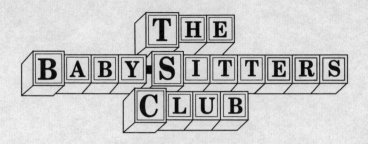

# CLAUDIA AND THE LITTLE LIAR

# Ann M. Martin

AN
**APPLE**
PAPERBACK

SCHOLASTIC INC.
New York Toronto London Auckland Sydney
Mexico City New Delhi Hong Kong

Cover art by Hodges Soileau

No part of this publication may be reproduced in whole or in part, or stored in a retrieval system, or transmitted in any form or by any means, electronic, mechanical, photocopying, recording, or otherwise, without written permission of the publisher. For information regarding permission, write to Scholastic Inc., Attention: Permissions Department, 555 Broadway, New York, NY 10012.

ISBN 0-590-50351-0

12 11 10 9 8 7 6 5 4 3 2 1     9/9 0 1 2 3 4/0

Printed in the U.S.A.     40

First Scholastic printing, March 1999

*The author gratefully acknowledges*
*Suzanne Weyn*
*for her help in*
*preparing this manuscript.*

# CLAUDIA AND THE
# LITTLE LIAR

# CHAPTER 1

I glanced at Josh as he sat on my bed and worked on his sewing. A small V-shaped wrinkle had formed in the center of his forehead and — without his realizing it — the tip of his tongue had crept out of the corner of his mouth.

In the months that we'd been going out, I'd come to learn that this adorable expression meant Josh Rocker was concentrating very hard on what he was doing. Unfortunately, I could also see that all his concern and thought hadn't prevented a big problem.

As if he sensed that I was watching him, Josh looked up. "What?" he asked, suddenly self-conscious.

"Sorry to mention this," I began, shifting uncomfortably in my director's chair, "but I think there might be a problem with the shirt you're sewing."

"There is?" he asked doubtfully, holding the

1

shirt out in front of him. It was a white T-shirt with a basketball-shaped badge in the right-hand corner. On the badge were the letters GSBA, which stands for Girls' Stoneybrook Basketball Association. GSBA is a local group of neighborhood girls here in Stoneybrook, Connecticut, who were inspired by the Women's National Basketball Association to start their own basketball league.

The girls involved are younger than my friends and me, who are in middle school. But we'd volunteered to help out, so I was decorating uniforms and Josh was helping me. We were getting started this afternoon by sewing on the badges I'd ordered from a print shop in downtown Stoneybrook.

"I think you've stitched the two sides of the shirt together," I said gently.

"No way," Josh protested, running his hand up the middle of the shirt. "Oops," he said with a quick grimace. Then he blushed slightly, the red spreading around his cheeks. (So cute.)

"That's okay." I reached behind me and took a pair of scissors from my desk. "Just snip it out and start again."

Rolling his eyes, Josh took the scissors from me.

The door opened and my sixteen-year-old sister, Janine, stuck her head in. "Is everything proceeding as planned in here?" she asked. "Do you require any assistance?"

Janine can be *such* a superbrain oddball. She's a real-life genius with a sky-high IQ. Josh and I couldn't help but smile at the way she talks like a brainiac, as if she's playing the part of a genius on a TV show.

We also smiled because we knew Janine was just pretending to care if we needed help. She was actually looking for an excuse to keep a close eye on Josh and me.

My parents expect Janine to be in charge when they're out. She takes that responsibility very seriously. And I know her well enough to be sure that my being alone with Josh was making her nervous

"Thanks, Janine, but we're fine," I assured her.

"That's excellent," she said. "If you need anything, I'll be in my room working on my calculus assignment." As she left, I noticed she pushed my door open even farther and left it that way.

I smiled to myself as I went back to my own sewing. Janine didn't have to be so worried. Sure, Josh and I were boyfriend and girlfriend — but we were also good friends. We like to do things when we're together rather than sit around and be romantic all the time. Of course we have our lovey-dovey moments, but they aren't the biggest part of our relationship.

"I can't believe this," Josh muttered as he picked at his stitches with the scissors blade. "This is the second time I'm pulling these out. The first time they looked too messy. Now I've sewn the shirt together. How do you get me into these things?"

"Kristy got us both into it," I replied. Kristy Thomas is a good friend of mine. She's also the president of the Baby-sitters Club. (I'm vice-president. I'll fill you in on the Baby-sitters Club, also known as the BSC, later.) Mostly what you need to know about Kristy is that she's a sports nut. She's even the coach of a little-kid softball team called Kristy's Krushers. So, being wild for sports, she was naturally very excited when she heard about the GSBA, and volunteered the BSC members to help.

I myself am not particularly wild for sports. It's not that I hate them — I just don't care about them. What I *do* love is art. Painting, sculpting, jewelry making, printmaking, you name it. If it's artistic, I want to get my hands into it, which is why I leaped at the chance to design the GSBA uniforms.

Since Kristy had agreed to be the GSBA coach, I checked my designs with her before going ahead. She rejected my first two concepts before settling on the third, which was white shorts and T-shirts with the basketball badges

4

and a small design of girls playing basketball stamped in the lower corner of the shorts. I don't usually like such plain clothing, but I knew it was the kind of thing Kristy would approve of. And it had a crisp, sporty look that was appealing.

"Kristy got us into this, but you volunteered us to work on the uniforms," Josh argued.

"I did not," I protested. "I said *I* would work on the uniforms. I didn't say you would. *You* were the one who offered to help."

"I had to. How else would I ever get to see you? You're always so busy baby-sitting or with your friends or doing some art project. At least this way I can look at you while I sew."

He glared in disgust at the rumpled shirt on his lap. "Maybe that's the problem. I should look at the shirt more and you less."

The poor, pathetic shirt was starting to look like a crumpled kite. "Maybe so," I agreed with a raised eyebrow. Then we both started laughing.

That's the great thing about our relationship. We find the same things funny. And sad and boring and interesting. We have so much in common, though I'd never have expected it when we first met.

I wouldn't know Josh at all if I hadn't been sent back to the seventh grade for awhile. You see, I've never been strong in my schoolwork. I

5

can't seem to work up the interest or enthusiasm that other people have for it. I used to do so badly in the eighth grade that my parents and teachers decided it might be best if I went back to the seventh grade and mastered that work before moving on.

Although, at first, I was embarrassed beyond belief, going back to seventh grade was a smart idea. A surprising thing happened when I returned to my old classes. For the first time in my life, I actually did well in school. I even experienced the thrill of bringing home a good report card.

Another unexpected thing occurred at that time. I made some new seventh-grade friends. This wasn't as unbelievable as my good grades, but it took me by surprise. I've had the same friends for so long that making new ones wasn't something I ever thought I'd do. Especially not younger friends.

Before I revisited seventh grade, I had exactly two non-eighth-grade friends. Mallory Pike and Jessica Ramsey, both eleven, are two years younger than I am. I became friends with them through the BSC. Other than that, I barely knew who the younger kids at SMS (Stoneybrook Middle School) were. But now I have three really close seventh-grade friends: Joanna Fried, Jeannie Kim, and Shira Epstein. Plus

Josh, of course, since he's a friend as well as a boyfriend.

That's how the two of us started — as friends. Then, little by little, I realized I felt closer to Josh than I did to my other seventh-grade boyfriend, Mark. Part of me couldn't believe I'd break up with Mark, who was so cool and cute. But that's what I did, because another part of me just wanted to be with the guy who made me feel comfortable and happy.

I noticed Josh studying the shorts piled on the end of my bed. "What are you thinking?" I asked as I pulled a bag of potato chips from behind my pillow. (The first time Josh saw me pull junk food from a hidden place in my room he laughed so hard he fell down. Now he's used to it. My parents don't like me to eat junk food, so my room is a treasure trove of hidden cellophane bags containing various sweet and salty treats.)

As he spoke, Josh dug into the chip bag I held out. "Would Kristy completely freak if you dyed the waistband on those shorts blue?" he asked thoughtfully. "You could let the dye bleed down the shorts a little. It might look cool."

I was impressed. I thought it would look good too. The design I'd planned to print on the shorts could be the same color as the waistband. (I would be carving the stamp design from raw potato and using deep blue fabric paint on it.)

"I think you're right. It might look excellent," I said to him. "Let's do it."

"Do we run it past Kristy or just go ahead?"

"I don't know," I admitted, glancing at the digital clock on my desk. "But speaking of Kristy, it's almost time for our BSC meeting. Everyone will be arriving in a few minutes. We'd better pack this stuff up."

Josh stuck his needle into the badge and loosely folded the shirt. "Gladly," he said. "Claudia, do you want to go to the movies this Saturday?"

"I do, but I can't. It's my father's birthday and we're taking him out to dinner."

"You can't miss your dad's birthday. No problem. We'll do it another time."

"Yeah, sorry," I said. And I *was* sorry. I felt bad that there never seemed to be enough time for Josh.

Kristy and Abby Stevenson walked into the room then. It was before five-thirty, our usual meeting time, but Kristy always comes early and Abby gets a ride with her, so she's early too. "Hey, Rock Man," Abby greeted Josh in her usual high-energy style. "How's it going?"

"That's what I'm doing — going," he

replied, grinning, gathering his schoolbooks from my bed.

"You don't have to. Why don't you stay and watch a meeting?" Kristy suggested.

"Thanks, but I can't." Josh gets jittery around some of my friends. I think it's because they're older.

I walked with him to my front door. "I'll see you in school tomorrow," I told him.

"Okay. I'll call you later, after dinner," he said, shifting awkwardly from foot to foot.

It seemed like the moment for a kiss.

But we didn't.

Josh punched me lightly on the arm and left. I stood there wondering why the moment had felt so awkward. It was probably because Abby and Kristy were around. Maybe. I wasn't convinced that was the reason, but I couldn't think of another.

# CHAPTER 2

"He's so cute," Abby commented when I got back to my room.

"It's too bad he always gets so nervous when he sees us," Kristy said, dropping into the director's chair.

"He likes you guys," I assured them. "It's just hard being the only seventh-grader with a bunch of eighth-graders."

"It doesn't bother Jessi," Kristy argued.

"What doesn't bother me?" Jessi Ramsey asked as she entered the room.

"Being younger than the rest of us," Abby replied, then filled her in.

"It didn't bother me because Mallory was with me," Jessi said. "And now I know everyone so well that it's fine. But if I'd met you guys without her, I might have been nervous too."

She sat on the rug in the spot where she always used to sit with Mallory, and it didn't look right to see her there by herself. It was strange, now that Mallory was gone.

Maybe I'd better back up, though, and tell you a bit about our club, and how it works, and who we are.

Awhile back, Kristy came up with the idea of forming a business that would allow parents to call one number at specific times and reach a group of qualified baby-sitters. She contacted Mary Anne Spier, our friend and neighbor, Stacey McGill, and me. We were the original members of the Baby-sitters Club. Since I have a phone and a private number, it made the most sense to meet here in my room. We put out fliers listing my number and told parents to call during our meeting times, every Monday, Wednesday, and Friday afternoon between five-thirty and six.

If ever an idea was marked for instant success this was it. Right away we were swamped with calls. It was soon clear we needed more help. We invited a new girl in town, Dawn Schafer, to join. Then we asked Jessi and Mallory to join as junior members. When Dawn moved to California, where she'd originally come from, Abby — the new girl in town — took her place.

The latest development is that Mallory has gone off to boarding school. We couldn't come up with anyone to replace her, so we're hoping we can all pick up the extra jobs. We're not yet sure if this is going to work out. Right now it seems as if we're all sitting an awful lot.

As I've mentioned, Kristy is our president. This isn't only because the club was her idea. She's also very devoted to running it. Her style can be overbearing sometimes. We don't really mind, though, because she's lots of fun. And we know that she's the one who keeps the club moving so smoothly.

Kristy has another quality that makes her a great president. Ideas come to her a mile a minute. We call her the Idea Machine. She's always thinking of some interesting project or finding a new way to make the club work more effectively.

For example, it was her idea to bring Kid-Kits to difficult sitting jobs. Each of us has a box filled with small toys, art supplies, games — anything that will interest a kid and make him or her more comfortable with us.

The club notebook was also her idea. That's a book in which we write about every sitting job we go on. Writing in it is a chore for most of us. (Especially for someone like me, who finds writing tough. Spelling totally baffles me. I'd rather draw a picture of what went on.) Reading the notebook is incredibly helpful, though. If we're going to sit for a family we haven't seen in awhile, we can simply read the book to find out what's happening with them.

While Kristy has tons of ideas about the BSC, she doesn't spend much mental energy on fashion. She always wears jeans, T-shirts or sweatshirts, and sneakers. Her long, light brown hair is straight and often covered by a team cap. She's the smallest girl in our grade, which just proves you can't always tell about a person from her appearance. Kristy may look small and plain, but she's not. A big personality lies inside.

Another thing you wouldn't guess about Kristy from looking at her is that she lives in a mansion. Her stepfather, Watson, is a millionaire. (Kristy's biological father abandoned the family when she was six.) When Mrs. Thomas married Watson, the whole family, including Kristy's two older brothers, Charlie and Sam, and her younger brother, David Michael, moved across town to Watson's. His kids from his first marriage, Karen and Andrew, live there part-time. (They live with their mother and her new husband when they're not at the mansion.) Kristy's mom and Watson also adopted a little girl, Emily Michelle, who was born in Vietnam. In order to help care for Emily Michelle, Kristy's grandmother, Nannie, moved into the house. Add a lot of pets to this mix and you have a very full house. Thank goodness it's a big one.

I've told you most of the things you need to know about me, except what I look like. I have long black hair and dark eyes, and I'm Japanese-American. In general, I'm pretty okay with my looks.

Since we meet in my room and use my phone, I tend to act as the club hostess. Being hostess is easy for me since, as I told you, my room comes fully stocked with treats, including something healthy for Stacey to eat.

"Hey, everybody!" Stacey walked in at 5:27. She glanced at the clock. "Wow, just made it. I stayed after school for Math Club and I didn't have time for a snack. Have you got anything, Claudia?"

Earlier that afternoon I'd cut up some carrots and celery. I handed them to her from my desk.

"Thanks, you're a pal," she said with a smile.

Of course I'm a pal. Stacey is my best friend. And I know how important it is that she eat right and not get hungry. She has to keep her blood-sugar level as regular as possible because she has diabetes, a condition in which her body can't properly regulate the amount of sugar in her blood. In addition, she has to give herself injections of something called insulin every day. She's made the injections and eating right a part of her life. She doesn't let her illness get her down or stop her from doing anything. I admire the way she handles it.

Stacey is our club treasurer. As you might have guessed from her mention of Math Club, she's a math whiz, so the job naturally fell to her. Every Monday she collects dues in a manila envelope. We all grumble as we hand over our money, but it's not a real complaint. We know dues paying is necessary. Stacey budgets the money so there's enough to help pay my phone bill and to restock the Kid-Kits when needed. We also pay Kristy's brother Charlie to drive Kristy (and often Abby) to meetings, since they don't live within walking distance. If there's ever any money left over, we use it for fun things, like treating ourselves to a pizza party.

You can easily tell that Stacey is originally from Manhattan. She has a big-city style. Unlike me — I like to put my outfits together in my own way, combining things I make with items I find on my treasure hunts in thrift shops — Stacey has a very pulled-together, fashion-forward look. And some boy or other is always paying attention to her. Now she dates this cute fifteen-year-old art student named Ethan, who lives in Manhattan. The distance isn't a problem since Stacey's in New York City a lot. She goes there often to visit her father. (Her parents are divorced.)

While Stacey was munching her carrots, Abby began to lift up pillows and move

15

around chairs. She turned to me, holding my latest Nancy Drew mystery in her hand. "I'm searching for Ring-Dings and all I've found so far is this," she said. (My parents don't think Nancy Drew mysteries are "intellectually stimulating" enough. So, like the treats, I hide them in my room.)

"Hmmm." I considered. "Ring-Dings . . . let me think." In a second I remembered, reached behind my dresser, and handed a box to her.

Abby opened it. "Thanks. It's just what I need to build up my strength for another hard half hour of alternating."

She was joking — something she does a lot. Her joke referred to the fact that she's our alternate officer. This means that she has to know how to do every job so that if someone is absent, she can take over. Most of the time, she doesn't have anything to do, since we're seldom absent. She's such a take-charge person that I think it frustrates her not to have a more active office. But instead of acting put out, she jokes about it.

Abby grew up on Long Island, in New York State. She recently moved into a big house with her mother and her twin sister, Anna. (Their father was killed in a car accident a few years ago.)

It's easy to tell Anna from Abby, even though they're identical twins. Abby wears her curly, dark hair long, while Anna's is short. They both need glasses, but they have different frames, and Abby tends to wear her contact lenses more than Anna does. Their energy styles are also different. Abby is always bouncing around, while Anna is more calm.

Abby is a sports person. She plays soccer and runs. Anna is a talented violinist who takes her playing very seriously.

They both have some health problems, but they're also different. Abby has lots of allergies. She says life makes her sneeze. Plus she has asthma and keeps an inhaler with her in case of an attack.

Anna was recently diagnosed as having scoliosis, which is a curvature of the spine. She'll have to wear a brace for the next few years in order to straighten out her spine. It's fitted especially to her body and worn under clothes, so you hardly notice it.

Anna and Abby rely on each other a lot since their mother works long hours as an executive editor for a big publishing company in New York. Often she's not home on weekends or for dinner because her job demands so much time. It's a good thing that Abby and Anna have each other.

"Why don't you cut it a little close, Mary Anne," Abby teased as Mary Anne ran into the room at exactly five-thirty. (Kristy insists we all be on time. Sometimes getting here by exactly five-thirty becomes a little stressful.)

"I wasn't worried," Mary Anne replied. "I have the walk from my house to Claudia's timed to the minute."

I knew Mary Anne was kidding, but I almost believed her about having timed the trip to my house. Being organized is one of her strong points. As club secretary she's in charge of our record book and has never made a mistake in it. This is a huge job.

When a client calls, the person nearest to the phone picks it up and takes down the client's request and information. Then she says she'll call right back and hangs up. From there, Mary Anne looks in the record book to see who's free to take the job.

Mary Anne has recorded everyone's schedule in the book. She knows when I have an art class and when Stacey is going to visit her father. If Kristy has a Krushers game or if Abby has an appointment with her allergist — it's recorded in the record book. Sometimes Mary Anne knows our schedules better than we do!

Once Mary Anne has figured out who is free to take the job, she offers it to one of us, based on how recently we've worked. She's always super-fair and no one ever has a complaint.

Mary Anne is not only fair, she's also extremely nice. Nice may sound boring, but I don't mean it that way, because she's not boring. She's a great listener and really cares about people. When someone has a problem, Mary Anne is so sensitive she sometimes bursts into tears. It's as if she shares the other person's pain.

I sometimes wonder if this quality comes from the fact that Mary Anne herself has known some hard times. Her mother died when Mary Anne was a baby. Soon after, Mary Anne was sent to live with her grandparents. They were very caring, but the time came when her father felt he was able to deal with raising her on his own. Then there was a legal fight over who should raise her. In the end, her father won.

He's been a great father but not an easy one. I remember when we were all younger here on Bradford Court (which is the name of the street where Kristy, Mary Anne, and I grew up). Mary Anne's father, Richard, had rules for everything. I guess it was his way of trying to be a good parent. He was so strict that he would have driven me crazy. By the time we were in the seventh grade, Mary Anne still looked like a little kid, with her hair in braids. She even had to wear these awful pleated skirts with white blouses.

Then an unexpected thing happened. Mary Anne became friendly with Dawn. Although they looked very different they were soul mates and quickly became best friends.

One day they browsed through Dawn's mother's high school yearbook and discovered that their parents were once sweethearts. Sharon, Dawn's mom, was originally from Stoneybrook but had gone to college in California and stayed there. Now, though, she was divorced from Dawn's dad and had come back to Stoneybrook, along with Dawn and Dawn's younger brother, Jeff.

Mary Anne and Dawn hatched a plan to get their parents back together. And it worked. Mary Anne and Dawn became stepsisters.

Unfortunately, Jeff had already returned to California. Mary Anne and Richard moved too, away from Bradford Court and into Dawn and Sharon's old farmhouse on Burnt Hill Road. Some time later, Dawn decided she wanted to return to California to live with her brother, her father, and her father's new wife. We were all sad (Mary Anne especially) that Dawn was leaving. Even though she comes back for vacations and is an honorary member of the BSC, it's not the same as when she was here all the time.

Luckily, Dawn didn't leave Mary Anne entirely alone. She has us, and she also has a boyfriend, Logan Bruno. He's also an associate member of the club. That means he doesn't come to meetings but we call him if we have more jobs than we can handle. If he's free — meaning if he's not busy with one of the many teams he's on — he'll take the job.

We have one other associate member. Her name is Shannon Kilbourne and she lives across the street from Kristy. Shannon attends Stoneybrook Day, a private school. The good thing about that is that if there's a school function we all want to go to, Shannon won't be involved in it and might be free to take a job.

The phone rang. It was one of our regular customers, Mrs. Braddock, wanting a sitter for Friday night. Mary Anne checked her book. "You're the only one free, Claudia," she informed me. "Want it?"

"Sure," I agreed. "Matt and Haley are always fun."

"Great," Mary Anne said as she wrote my name in the record book. When she was done writing, she glanced at Jessi. "Are you okay?" she asked softly.

I saw why she was concerned. Jessi was sitting on the rug, her chin propped on her hand, keeping quiet and looking glum. If anyone could understand how it felt to lose a best friend, Mary Anne could. That's exactly what had happened to Jessi. As I mentioned, her best friend, Mallory, had departed for Riverbend, a private boarding school in Massachusetts. As with Dawn, she'd remain an honorary member, but it wouldn't be the same.

"Club meetings are the hardest," Jessi said. "Otherwise I'm too busy to feel very lonely."

Jessi is truly a busy person. She's a talented ballet student who takes classes in Stamford, the closest city to Stoneybrook. Because Jessi is eleven, she's a junior officer, which means she takes only afternoon jobs during the week, or evening jobs for her own family.

"Hey, Claud, these uniforms are going to look great," Kristy said, picking up one of the shirts from the bed. "I love that they're so simple and sporty."

"Thanks," I said, nodding. It was almost as if she knew I was planning a tie-dye waistband and was telling me not to do it.

"What happened to this one?" Abby asked, picking up the shirt Josh had more or less mangled.

"Oh," I replied with a smile, "Josh has been helping me. Sometimes his help is not so helpful."

"Oh, but it's so cute of him to try," Mary Anne said.

"He's really adorable," Jessi added.

I smiled at them, appreciating their praise. But they made it sound as if Josh were a puppy instead of a guy. I wasn't sure that was a good thing.

# CHAPTER 3

It's not far to the Braddocks' house from mine. On Friday I arrived right after our BSC meeting, at 6:05. (The Kristy influence is wearing off on me. I'm starting to tell time in exact minutes.)

Seven-year-old Matt peeked out the front window and then opened the door for me. With a quick wave of his hand, he shaped his fingers into the American Sign Language symbol for "Hi," and I returned it. Matt attends the School for the Deaf in Stamford. He's been profoundly deaf since birth.

Because we sit for him, everyone in the BSC has learned a little sign language. Jessi knows more than the rest of us because when Mrs. Braddock first began using us as sitters she taught Jessi some signs and Jessi was fascinated and wanted to learn more.

I probably know the least since I'm so bad with vocabulary. But nine-year-old Haley Braddock is a whiz at sign language and she's usually willing to interpret for me.

"Hi, Claudia," Haley greeted me as she came bouncing down the stairs.

Mrs. Braddock came in from the kitchen. "Oh, great, Claudia, you're here. How are you?"

"Fine." I turned to Haley. "I've been working on the uniforms for your team."

"Awesome!" she cried. Haley was one of the girls in the GSBA.

"Would you like a blue waistband or a plain one?" I asked.

"Whatever," she said with a shrug. Not much help there.

Mrs. Braddock called up the stairs to her husband, telling him I'd arrived. Then she went to the front hall closet for her jacket. "We'll just be at the elementary school for a meeting of the spring dance committee. We shouldn't be much past nine at the latest," she told me. She pulled on her jacket as Mr. Braddock came downstairs and took his from the closet.

"Oh, and Haley," Mrs. Braddock said, pulling open the front door, "make sure you do your homework."

"But Mom, it's Friday!" Haley protested. "I have all weekend."

"We talked about this, Haley," Mr. Braddock

said firmly. "Remember, we agreed to get homework out of the way on Friday so we don't have any more Sunday night panics."

"Oh, all right," Haley grumbled.

"No TV until she does it," Mrs. Braddock told me.

"Okay," I agreed. I hated having to enforce a tough rule, but I was there to do what the Braddocks asked.

Almost the very moment they left, Haley snapped on the TV. She plunked herself down on the living room sofa next to Matt and began to watch. "Sorry, Haley," I said, "but you have to do your homework."

"You're not going to really make me, are you?" she asked.

"I don't have any choice."

"Sure you do. You can let me watch TV for awhile, and then I'll do my homework."

I hated this kind of argument. It made me feel like some kind of authority figure, and that's not a position I like being in. I'd rather be friendly and make sure the kids don't get themselves into trouble. But I was stuck with an authority role and I had to be responsible.

"Haley," I insisted, "*please* do your homework."

She twisted her face into an expression combining exasperation and disgust. "I can't believe you're making me do this," she grumbled, dragging herself up the stairs to her room.

As I sighed, Matt tapped my shoulder. He waved me to follow him to the TV and held up a new video game he'd gotten. It had just come out and had amazing graphics. He pointed back and forth between himself and me. I understood that he wanted to show me how to play.

I nodded and smiled, taking a seat on the floor in front of the TV. I watched as Matt showed off his skills at driving his video cart around sharp turns and over hazards. Then I struggled to learn what to do as he patiently showed me how to maneuver the controls. For about an hour it was wipeout city, I'm afraid.

After a particularly awful crash, I decided I needed a break. Handing the controls to Matt, I signaled that I'd be right back and strolled into the kitchen for some soda.

On my way to the refrigerator, I noticed that one of the lights on the Braddocks' wall phone was lit. That indicated that someone was talking on one of their two phone lines. That someone could only be Haley.

It was possible she was only making a quick homework-related call. It was also possible that she'd been chatting on the phone from the minute she went upstairs. I figured I'd better find out which it was.

26

Maybe it was sneaky, but I stood outside her door for a moment before knocking. It told me all I needed to know.

"Can you believe it, Vanessa?" I heard her say. "I can't wait until the movie opens. It stars all three of those guys, and they sing. I didn't even know they had a band. Have you ever heard them sing? Me neither!"

This didn't sound like a homework conversation. It sounded like nattering with her best friend, Vanessa Pike.

I knocked on the door. Haley was suddenly silent. "Come . . . come in," she said in an unsteady voice.

When I stepped inside, I found Haley sitting cross-legged on the end of her bed, holding a cordless phone to her ear. Upon seeing me, she changed her casual tone to one of serious formality. "That equation sounds right," she said into the phone. "Thanks for your help on this math. I couldn't have done it without you, Vanessa." She listened as Vanessa spoke. "Oh, Claudia is here now, so I'll have to go."

I tried not to smile. I knew the "Claudia is here" part was to explain why she'd switched gears so abruptly.

She clicked off the cordless phone and set it beside her on the bed. "Vanessa was helping me with math," she said. One glance around her room told me there wasn't a math text or notebook in sight. I didn't want to make a huge deal over it, though.

"What homework have you got?" I asked.

"Now that the math is done," she said, going to her desk on which sat a computer, "all I have to do is write my monthly book report."

"Do you need help?" I offered.

She shook her head. "No. I started it before I called Vanessa. I only have to write a few more sentences."

"Okay. Let me see it when you're done."

"Mom didn't say you had to check my homework," Haley protested.

"I know, but I have to be sure it's done," I explained.

She pouted and folded her arms. "Why are you taking this so seriously, Claudia?"

This was a new tone of voice for Haley. It was more grown-up — in an unpleasant sort of way.

"Your mother asked me to make sure you did your homework," I said. "Matt and I aren't even watching TV," I added. "We're playing a video game. When you're done, we'll turn on the TV and we can all watch it together."

Back downstairs, I played the video game with Matt for another fifteen minutes. Then Haley appeared with several papers in her hand. "My report," she announced, handing the papers to me.

"*The Great Brain*," I said, reading the title of the book she'd reported on. Flipping through, I saw the report was neatly typed. The little I read seemed sensible and even enthusiastic. "Looks good to me," I said, handing it back to her. "That's all you have to do?"

"That's all," she replied, picking up the TV remote control. "Now can we watch TV?" She stepped in front of Matt and signed to him. I assumed she was asking him the same thing.

He made a face and shook his head. Obviously he wasn't done playing his video game.

She signed some more and his expression brightened. He snapped off the video game and turned on the TV. "Matt almost forgot that his favorite movie is on tonight," Haley explained.

The three of us settled in on the couch to watch. The movie was nearly over when the Braddocks returned home. "Well, it looks like everything is calm enough here," Mr. Braddock commented as he pulled off his jacket and hung it up in the hall closet.

"Is your homework done?" Mrs. Braddock asked Haley.

"Yup," she replied, her eyes still on the TV.

"Her report on *The Great Brain* is right over there on the table," I added.

Haley turned from the TV and looked at me sharply.

Mrs. Braddock frowned.

I was confused.

"Haley, this isn't the same report on *The Great Brain* that you did last month . . . is it?" Mrs. Braddock asked sternly.

Uh-oh. From the trapped look on Haley's face, I suddenly knew what had happened. Haley had simply printed out last month's report, figuring she'd fool me and then watch TV.

"Haley! How could you do such a deceitful thing?" Mrs. Braddock scolded.

"I'll do the report," Haley insisted huffily. "I just didn't want to do it tonight."

Mr. Braddock returned from hanging up his coat. "Haley," he said in a firm "Dad" voice. "Go upstairs and do your report right now."

"Thanks a lot, Claudia," Haley snapped at me, her arms folded angrily. "If you hadn't turned me in, everything would have been fine."

"That's enough, Haley," Mrs. Braddock warned her. "Go to your room."

As Haley stormed off, Mrs. Braddock turned to me, wearing an apologetic expression. "I don't know what's gotten into her lately."

"It's okay," I said, standing up. "I'm sorry I didn't realize about the report."

"There was no way for you to know," Mrs.

Braddock assured me. "This is entirely Haley's fault."

I knew that was true, but I wondered if Haley saw it that way. Somehow, I strongly suspected she didn't.

# CHAPTER 4

Saturday

Claudia, you're my best friend. But you owe me one this time. If you get a member of the basketball team grounded, please do it on a day when I won't have to fill in for her.

Stacey wasn't actually baby-sitting that Saturday afternoon. At least she wasn't being paid for it. Kristy had volunteered her to help out with the girls' basketball team that afternoon in the Stoneybrook Elementary School gym.

Like me, Stacey isn't terribly involved in sports. She likes to bike and swim and that sort of thing, but she's no superathlete.

Still, she didn't mind helping out. She figured Kristy would do the coaching part. All Stacey would have to do was show up and lend a hand.

Little did she know!

"Haley can't come today," Vanessa announced the moment she walked into the gym. "She's been grounded."

"For how long?" Kristy asked. She could already figure out *why* Haley had been grounded, since I'd told my friends the story about her homework that morning on the phone.

Vanessa shrugged. "I don't know."

Kristy turned, looked at her players, and did a quick count. "I'm one short," she said. "Now what?" That's when her gaze fell on Stacey. "You'll have to play."

"Excuse me?"

"Come on, Stacey, you have to," Kristy

pleaded. "You can't let down the rest of the girls."

"Me? Why don't *you* play?"

"I can't coach and play at the same time."

Stacey couldn't argue with that, so she joined the other girls.

She already knew a bunch of them from baby-sitting. Besides Vanessa, Jessi's younger sister, Becca, was there. So were Charlotte Johanssen, Karen Brewer (Kristy's stepsister), and Sara Hill, along with some eight- and nine-year-olds Stacey didn't know as well.

Charlotte wrapped her arms around Stacey. "Oh, I'm so glad you're on my team," she squealed. Stacey is by far Charlotte's favorite sitter.

"Just for now," Stacey reminded her.

"Stacey, no offense, but . . . aren't you a little tall to be playing with us?" Becca asked.

Stacey laughed. "I sure am," she agreed.

Kristy wasted no time in separating the girls into two practice teams. The girls on the team without Stacey instantly protested. "We can't win with her on their team," Vanessa pointed out. "No matter what position she plays, it will give them an advantage."

"This is just a practice," Kristy replied with a touch of annoyance in her voice. "It doesn't matter who wins."

"It matters to us," Vanessa insisted sulkily. "Why play if you can't win?"

"Believe me, I'm not a great player," Stacey assured her. "You probably have a better chance of winning without me on your team."

The girls on Stacey's team groaned. "Thanks for telling us," Sara said.

Kristy blew her whistle loudly. "No more arguing. Let's play." She assigned Stacey to be a guard, which caused a lot of grumbling.

"Nothing like having a giant guarding you," a girl named Diana Gonzalez complained when Stacey stole the ball from her.

"Sorry," Stacey apologized. "I'm just doing my guard job."

Stacey felt more than a little ridiculous. She towered over everyone. And, despite not being the ultimate sportswoman, she'd been playing basketball longer than most of the other girls had been alive.

Then there was the Kristy factor. It seemed that every other minute Stacey heard a whistle blaring in her ear. "McGill! Traveling!" Kristy shouted, circling her arms around each other to indicate Stacey's breach of the rules.

It took Stacey a second to remember that traveling meant she was running with the ball. "Get off it! I was not," she argued.

"McGill, you're benched for talking back to the coach," Kristy told her.

Stacey's jaw dropped. She couldn't believe Kristy was actually benching her. "You can't bench me. You have no one to replace me with."

"You're right," Kristy had to agree. "I'll have to give the other team a free throw instead." This news brought forth an assortment of cheers and groans.

Throughout the remainder of the game, Kristy continued to be especially hard on Stacey. By the end, Stacey was ready to strangle her.

"I was only trying to make things fair, since you had such an advantage over the other girls," Kristy whispered to her after the game was over and Stacey's team had lost.

Kristy ended the practice with a pep talk. "That was a good game, but you girls have a lot to learn. You have to share the ball more, and there were too many violations of the rules."

"Stacey made most of them," Sara pointed out.

"Well, I was a tougher on her because she should know better," Kristy said.

"There won't be so many mistakes once Haley comes back," Vanessa said.

Stacey wasn't sure she appreciated that.

"What's she grounded for, anyway?" Becca asked.

Vanessa jumped in. "Claudia told her parents that she didn't do her homework on Friday night. They were all upset even though Haley had the entire weekend to get it done. Claudia just did it to get her in trouble."

"Claudia wouldn't do that!" Charlotte said.

"No, she wouldn't," Stacey agreed.

"And even if she did, it wasn't to be mean. Claudia was only following the rules," Kristy added.

"See, Kristy admits it," Vanessa insisted. "Claudia *did* turn Haley in."

"That's not true," Stacey cried. "Claudia told me the whole story. Haley simply got caught in a lie. Claudia very innocently, by accident, told Haley's parents that Haley didn't do the book report."

*"Claudia told Haley's parents that Haley didn't do the book report,"* Vanessa echoed. "See? That's what I've been saying."

"You can't trust anyone over nine," Sara said with a sigh. "Once a kid becomes a two-digit number, something changes."

"Hey!" Diana objected. "That's not true. I'll be ten soon. The problem is baby-sitters. They're paid by parents, so that's who they're loyal to."

"No, the problem is Claudia," Vanessa disagreed. "She's turned on us."

I shook my head as Stacey told me this story later that Saturday. Even though I'd done nothing to deserve it, it seemed that I was getting a bad reputation among Haley and her pals.

# CHAPTER 5

**W**hile Stacey was playing basketball that Saturday afternoon, I was home, dyeing the waistbands of the team's shorts blue. I hadn't asked Kristy about this. I just went ahead and did it because I couldn't help myself. They'd look so cool. And, after all, wasn't I in charge of designing the uniforms?

I spread an old sheet on the grass in our backyard and then set the dyed shorts out to dry. The plastic gloves I wore were entirely blue. I peeled them off and threw them into the garbage. As I did, my dad wandered into the yard. Although it was late afternoon, this was the first time I'd seen him that day, since he'd gone out early before I awoke.

"Happy birthday, Dad!" I greeted him.

He smiled but shook his head. "Next Saturday," he said.

Oops.

"You mean it's not today?" I gasped. I'd been *so sure. . . .*

"No. I have one week left before I'm officially one year older. Don't rush me."

He looked at the team's shorts and said he liked them, but I'd have to move them because he was about to mow the lawn. As I dragged my sheet to the driveway, I realized I was now free to go to the movies with Josh. There was still time to call him.

I wasn't sure I wanted to go out, though. It's unusual for me to have a Saturday night when I'm not either baby-sitting or doing something with my friends or Josh. I could do my homework, which would leave all of Sunday free. (I'm usually terrible about leaving things to the last minute.)

There was also a Nancy Drew mystery I wanted to read — *The Case of the Artful Crime.* From the cover, I knew it was about clues hidden in paintings, so, as you might guess, I was especially eager to get to it. A Nancy Drew about art . . . what could be better?

I decided not to decide.

Not right away, anyhow. I'd do some homework, read for awhile, and then see how I felt about calling Josh. It wasn't as though he were expecting me to call.

It might not surprise you to hear that when I got to my room, I decided to read my book first and think about homework later. I located a bag of Cheez Doodles under my bed and *The Case of the Artful Crime* under my pillow, stretched out, ripped open the Cheez Doodles bag, and turned to page one of the book.

Heaven.

In minutes, I was lost in the story. Nancy had to track down a person who was buying lots of paintings. She realized that each painting contained a piece of information. Like pieces in a puzzle, the thief needed all the paintings in order to figure out where some priceless statue was buried. I loved it.

I forgot about time as I flew through the book. Hours passed, though I was hardly aware of it. I'd come to a scene in which Nancy was stuck in a room with the thief when . . . my phone rang. The sound startled me so much that I dropped the book. It took a moment for me to remember that I was Claudia in my room and not Nancy hiding behind a priceless tapestry.

"Hello?" I said foggily, snapping up the phone.

"Claudia, you're home."

Josh's voice was unmistakable to me.

"Uh . . . yeah," I replied.

"I thought you were going out with your family tonight," he said. I checked the time. It was seven o'clock. Wow! I had no idea. Normally someone would have called me for dinner by now, but I guess my parents were also running late.

I realized that it must seem odd that I was home when I said I wouldn't be, but something else was strange. "Why did you call me if you didn't think I was home?" I asked.

"I wanted to leave a message on your answering machine," Josh explained.

"Oh."

"Well, why are you home? Are you sick or something?"

That's so like Josh, immediately worried that I might not be okay. "No, I'm fine," I assured him. It suddenly seemed so dumb to say I got the date of my father's birthday wrong. "Um . . . Dad wasn't feeling well, so we're going to celebrate his birthday next week," I told him.

"That's too bad. What's the matter with him?"

"Some kind of bug. It probably won't last too long. He just now decided he was too ill to go and I figured it was too late to go to the movies."

"I hope you don't get whatever he's got." Josh's voice was genuinely concerned.

I wished he would drop the subject. The nicer he was, the worse I felt about not calling him earlier and about lying to him now.

"What message were you going to leave me?" I asked.

"I was wondering if you'd want to see the movie tomorrow. I thought it stopped playing on Saturday but I just looked in the paper and saw it's still there tomorrow," he said.

"Sure."

"Great. My dad will drive. I'll come by around three. Oh, and tell your dad I hope he feels better."

"What? . . . Oh, yeah, sure. I will."

On Sunday, when Josh arrived, I felt awfully guilty. I knew the lie I'd told was harmless, but I couldn't figure out why I hadn't simply admitted the truth.

Of course, if I told him the truth, I'd then have to explain why I hadn't called him the moment I realized my mistake.

Why hadn't I?

I wasn't sure. It was probably that I just preferred to stay home and read that night. But is that how you're supposed to feel when you're crazy about someone? It wasn't the kind of behavior you see on TV or in romantic movies.

No, it was better that I'd said what I did. It had made my life easier and it hadn't hurt Josh's feelings.

Just after Josh arrived, I heard my dad moving around on the second-floor landing. The moment I heard his foot on the stairs, I grabbed Josh's arm and hurried him toward the door. " 'Bye, Mom, Dad," I called over my shoulder.

Mom stepped out of the kitchen and waved. "Have fun."

"Remember, we're expecting you home for dinner," Dad called from the stairs.

"I remember," I called as I yanked open the door and practically pushed Josh out.

"Why are you in such a hurry?" Josh asked.

I shrugged and smiled nervously. "I don't want to miss the beginning of the movie. I hate that."

"We have plenty of time," Josh told me as we walked toward his father's car.

We slid into the backseat together. I said hi to Mr. Rocker, but after that, I didn't know what else to say. It was the weirdest feeling — almost as if I expected Josh to say, at any moment, that he knew I'd lied to him.

It didn't take long for me to realize it was only my guilt that was making me so uneasy. Josh wasn't doing or saying anything to make me think he was angry or suspicious.

By the time we arrived inside the theater, I'd relaxed a lot. That was the good news. The bad news was that the movie stunk.

But even *that* wasn't totally terrible. The acting was so bad and the plot made so little sense that it was hysterical, even though it wasn't meant to be funny.

The theater was pretty empty, so we didn't disturb anyone by laughing and commenting through the whole show. Josh can be pretty funny once he gets going. By the time the end credits came on, I was breathless with laughter.

It was a good feeling, but I noticed something about it. The feeling was almost too relaxed and natural. When I used to go to the movies with Mark, I would be thrilled just to be sitting next to him. If he held my hand, or even if our arms brushed against each other, it was as exciting as anything happening on the screen.

I never felt that way with Josh. Don't get me wrong — we've kissed, and he's a great kisser. But being with him felt as easy as being with any of my girlfriends. We were so comfortable together.

I wasn't sure it was the feeling I wanted when I was out with the boy I was supposed to feel romantic toward.

What could I do about it, though? Was there a way to change it?

I had no idea.

# CHAPTER 6

At our Monday meeting, Mrs. Braddock called, sounding slightly panicked. "I know it's short notice but I really need a sitter tonight," she said when I picked up the phone.

"I'm sure we can find someone for you," I assured her.

After I hung up and ran the job past Mary Anne, I made a request. "I'd really like to take it if no one else minds," I said.

"You would?" Stacey asked.

"Yeah. I want to straighten things out with Haley," I explained. "She and I have always gotten along well. I don't want this problem to get out of hand."

"That's a good idea," Kristy agreed. "Is it all right with everyone if Claudia takes the job?"

My friends said it was fine, so I called Mrs. Braddock back and made arrangements. Then after the meeting, I grabbed my backpack with my homework inside and headed over to the

Braddocks' house, which isn't far from my home.

"Thank you for coming, Claudia," Mrs. Braddock greeted me at the door. Haley wasn't around, but she lowered her voice just the same. "A friend of mine needs a lift to the hospital to visit her daughter. Her car broke down this afternoon. I'd rather not have Haley and Matt sitting around in a hospital waiting room if it's not necessary. Normally Mr. Braddock could stay home with them but he's working late."

"No problem," I told her with a smile. "All I have to do tonight is homework, which I can do here."

"Speaking of homework," Mrs. Braddock said, "please make sure Haley does hers. No TV until she completes it. She's been grounded not only because of the fake report, but because of other times she hasn't done her homework and then lied about it."

"Okay," I agreed.

"Thanks," she said and then called up the stairs. "Kids, I'm going!"

Haley and Matt ran down to say good-bye to her. Matt saw me and signed "Hi." Haley looked me over icily.

"Hi, guys," I greeted them. "Did you eat yet?"

Matt nodded. Haley ignored me and

dropped onto the couch, TV remote in hand.

"Your mom wants all homework done before TV," I said, trying to sound as cheerful as possible. "I have homework too. Why don't the three of us do it together?"

Haley rolled her eyes disdainfully . . . but she didn't turn on the TV. "Matt needs help with his homework," she said. "Why don't you help him down here and I'll do mine by myself," she suggested.

I turned toward Matt. "What do you have to do?"

He shook his head and waved his hands, indicating that he didn't have homework. Haley signed something to him and he signed back, shaking his head as he moved his hands.

"He's lying," Haley said to me. "He claims he doesn't have any homework, but he does."

"Do you have homework, Matt?" I asked. As I spoke, I pointed to my backpack to make my point.

He shook his head vigorously.

At that moment, the phone rang and Haley ran into the kitchen to answer it.

I wasn't sure who to trust. Had Matt caught the lying bug from Haley? Or was he telling the truth? Could Haley be trying to get him into trouble in order to take the heat off herself? I just didn't know.

Matt had never lied to me. I decided to trust

him. He was only seven. It was very possible that he didn't have homework.

My stomach grumbled, reminding me I hadn't eaten supper. I headed toward the kitchen to make myself a sandwich. As I approached I heard Haley talking on the kitchen phone. She mentioned the caller's name — Vanessa. I made a peanut butter and jelly sandwich while Haley talked. I figured I'd give her a few minutes to wrap it up. But she was still going strong when I'd finished making the sandwich and poured a glass of milk.

"Homework," I mouthed to Haley. I know she understood what I meant, but she turned her head away from me and stayed on the phone.

This was not a good sign. I didn't want to rip the phone out of her hand, but I wasn't going to be ignored either.

Then I had an idea. I went upstairs to Mr. and Mrs. Braddock's room and picked up their cordless phone, punching into the phone line that Haley was talking on. "Vanessa, hi, this is Claudia," I said, cutting into their conversation. "Haley has to do her homework now, so you'll have to end this conversation. She'll call you back when she's finished."

"All right," Vanessa replied sulkily. "I'd better go, Haley. I wouldn't want her to get you in trouble again. 'Bye."

I hung up but kept my eye on the phone's red light. In less than a minute, it went off.

As I headed down the stairs, I met Haley, who was walking up. "I'm going to do my homework now," she said in a snippy, irritated voice.

"Okay, call me if you need any help," I replied, ignoring her tone.

"Not likely," she muttered as she disappeared into her room.

While Haley worked (or so I hoped), I ate my supper, then played Go Fish with Matt. I was glad we'd found an activity that didn't involve the TV. Turning it on might have seemed as if we were tormenting Haley for not being able to watch.

After an hour or so, Haley came downstairs with several sheets of paper and a notebook. "This is a math fill-in sheet. And that paper is my written response to a story we read in class today. And in my notebook are some questions about the Antarctic I had to answer." She handed me another paper with her homework assignment typed on it. "My teacher sends this home now so my parents know exactly what homework I have," she explained coolly. "You can see it's all done."

Glancing at the assignment sheet, I saw that it was all there. "Terrific," I said, smiling. "That wasn't so bad, was it?"

"It was bad enough," she muttered.

"Aw, come on," I coaxed. "I hate doing my homework too, but everyone has to do it. I know it doesn't seem very important, but it must have a purpose or they wouldn't give it to you."

"Its purpose is to wreck our evenings and weekends," Haley stated flatly.

There were times I'd thought that myself, but it didn't seem helpful to admit it just then. Like it or not, homework is given to you and it has to be done. There isn't much point in not doing it because that creates more problems than it's worth. In the end, it's easier just to do it and get it over with.

"*Now* can I call Vanessa?" Haley asked.

"Sure. Go ahead," I told her. She went into the kitchen and phoned Vanessa.

Matt picked up *TV Guide* and pointed to a show he wanted to watch. I turned on the TV and we watched together. The Braddocks have closed-captioned TV. Any spoken words are written on the screen. That way Matt can read them and know what's being said. I bet it helps him be a good reader. I read along — just to see what it was like — and sometimes I had to read pretty fast.

In about fifteen minutes, I decided to get us each a soda. As I approached the kitchen, I could hear Haley, still on the phone.

"Yeah, Matt and the traitor are watching something on TV now," she was saying. "No, she can't hear me with the television on."

*The traitor?* That hurt. Was that how she thought of me now?

Obviously it was.

"The little tattletale made me do every drop of homework and then she checked it against the assignment sheet," Haley went on. "Can you believe that? Claudia used to be so cool. Now she's changed."

Had I changed? I didn't think so. It was Haley who had changed. *The little tattletale.* That was cold.

I changed my mind about the soda and returned to the living room. I was stunned. I couldn't remember a sitting charge ever being so hostile toward me. For an hour or two, sure. But not for days. It was especially bizarre coming from Haley, whom I'd known for so long. Vanessa seemed to be angry with me too. I'd known her just as long and as well as I'd known Haley.

I tried to brush the incident off. Haley was just having some problems at school and it was easier to blame me than to look at the real issues. Vanessa was her best friend, so naturally she'd side with Haley. Logically, it was nothing to be upset about. I couldn't help it, though.

The plain fact was that my feelings had been hurt.

Still . . . I reminded myself that I was the older and more mature person here. I'd rise above it and pretend I hadn't heard what I'd heard. If I ignored it, the problem would probably just go away on its own.

With that in mind, I acted cheerful and positive when I saw Haley again, even though she ignored me and spent most of the time in her room. When Mrs. Braddock returned around 8:30 Matt jumped up to greet her. She kissed him and told him to start getting ready for bed.

"Haley did every bit of her homework," I reported as Matt went up the stairs.

"Good," Mrs. Braddock said. "Haley," she called up the stairs. Haley came right down to the living room. "Claudia says your homework is done," her mother began.

"Yes, no thanks to her," Haley said.

My jaw dropped. "Excuse me?" I said.

"You kept blabbing on the phone to Vanessa, interrupting while I was trying to go over the math with her," she said.

I thought I was stunned before. Now I was out-and-out astounded. How could she say this?

"Haley, you know I just got on the line to get you off the phone," I said.

"Yeah, right," Haley scoffed. "That's not too believable since you told me you don't even think homework is important."

I looked at Mrs. Braddock, desperately hoping she wouldn't believe this. "I told her that sometimes homework doesn't *seem* important, but it has to be done," I said.

"That's not what I heard," Haley insisted.

"Enough, Haley," said Mrs. Braddock.

Haley glared at me. Then she stomped out of the living room and up the stairs.

"I'm sorry about Haley," Mrs. Braddock apologized as she took money from her wallet. "Suddenly she's become a handful. Her father and I aren't sure what to do."

Mr. Braddock came in then and offered to drive me home. I said I could walk, but since it was dark, he insisted.

In minutes, I was back at my own doorstep, happy to be away from Haley. She was certainly becoming quite a little liar. She'd lied about Matt's having homework. And she'd lied about me to her mother — in front of my face!

For some reason, she'd singled me out to be the object of her lies. And I didn't like it one bit.

"This is serious," Kristy said the next day at lunch. As usual, all the older BSC members were sitting at the same table. I'd just finished telling my friends what had happened the night before at the Braddocks'.

"What if all the kids we sit for start telling lies about us?" Kristy went on.

"That's not going to happen," Stacey said. "Our kids wouldn't do that."

"Haley has," Kristy insisted.

"That's Haley," Abby argued. "The rest of the kids aren't like that."

"She's already gotten to Vanessa," Kristy reminded us. "I saw Haley and Vanessa talking to Becca and some of the other girls at practice last Saturday. Even if they don't all start lying, they could spread the lies Haley has been telling. Suppose Becca goes home and says Claudia told Haley homework isn't important. Mrs. Ramsey might think twice about asking us to sit for Becca and Squirt." (Squirt is Jessi's little brother.)

"Mrs. Ramsey would know better than to believe something like that," said Mary Anne.

"Okay, maybe she would, since her daughter is a BSC member, but other parents might not," Kristy said. "They were talking to Sara Hill too. Her parents don't know us as well as some of our other clients."

Kristy has a way of worrying about things the rest of us don't even think about. She insists on punctuality partly because we're only at meetings for a half hour, but also because she frets that if we start coming late to meetings, we'll also show up late for jobs, and then customers will get fed up and stop calling. It's just how her mind works.

In a way, I thought that she was making too big a deal over the Haley situation. Then again she might be right. Lies do have a way of spreading and causing even bigger problems. "What do you think we should do about it?" I asked her.

"I don't know," she said, sitting back in her chair with a serious, thoughtful expression on her face. "But I'm going to watch Haley closely at basketball practice this afternoon."

Josh and I had made plans to hang out together after school that Tuesday. Since he'd been complaining that he didn't see enough of me, I felt I should make some time for him. We had no exact plan — only to be together.

"Ready?" he asked, coming to my locker at dismissal.

"Yup," I replied as I pulled my backpack over one shoulder. We strolled down the hall together, not talking. It was odd, as if we'd run out of things to say.

I began searching my brain for something to talk about. I didn't really want to tell him about Haley. I wanted to take a break from thinking about her for awhile. But I couldn't come up with anything else. "You won't believe what happened while I was sitting yesterday," I began.

He listened as I told him the story. Just talking about it made me feel upset all over again. Something else was bothering me too.

Josh.

I didn't feel that I had his undivided attention. He appeared to be listening, but it was as if he were thinking about something other than what I was saying. There was a faraway look in his eye, and he didn't comment at all.

"Are you listening to me?" I demanded as we walked out of the school building.

"Yes," he replied. He looked surprised that I'd asked.

"You're not saying anything," I pointed out.

"That's because I'm listening."

That made sense, I supposed, so I continued my story. But I couldn't figure out Josh's reaction. Normally he'd be making comments, jokes, observations. He wasn't the type to listen without jumping in at certain points in the conversation.

I remembered a science fiction movie I'd seen called *Invasion of the Body Snatchers*. Giant pods from outer space took over people's bodies while they slept. You could tell when a pod had gotten someone because the person's behavior changed.

Between Haley and Josh, I was beginning to suspect we'd had a pod invasion recently.

"So, what do you suggest?" I asked him when I had finished my story. "Do you have any idea why she's changed so much?"

"Who knows?" he said with a shrug.

This was definitely not Josh. Normal Josh would have come up with a million possibilities and theories.

"Did you even hear what I said?"

"Yeah, some bratty little kid is driving you nuts because she's lying her head off."

"Well, sort of," I agreed. "But it's more than that. This is a girl I know and used to get along with. It upsets me that she's acting this way."

"Forget about her," he suggested.

"I can't. She's ruining my reputation with

some of the other kids, and Kristy's even worried that the things she's saying might hurt the entire BSC."

He shook his head, disbelieving. "No way. I think you're making too much out of this. Blow it off."

"I could try to, I guess," I said quietly. It seemed to me that Josh just couldn't be bothered thinking about this problem. Maybe something bigger was on his mind. "Are you okay?" I asked. "Is everything all right?"

"Yeah, I'm fine," he answered.

We decided to walk to Brenner Field and sit on the big rock at its edge. There was no real reason to go there, but at least it was a destination.

It was one of those super-windy March days that I really love. The trees were bending in the wind, and stuff from the streets was blowing around us. Josh tugged down on his baseball cap as the wind nearly lifted it from his head.

As we walked, my mind raced, searching for an answer to the question of what was wrong with Josh. I didn't believe that he was fine.

By the time we were near the field, I had come to the conclusion that the problem had to be me. What else could it have been? If it had been something else, he would have told me about it.

In the field, out on the baseball diamond,

some kids were flying kites. One was in the shape of a dragon with a long tail that danced in the air. "That's so cool, isn't it?" I commented as we climbed the rock together up to the flat part where we could sit comfortably.

"Yeah, it is," he agreed. "Hey, do you want to try to make a kite together?"

"Sure. I've never done it, have you?"

"Once. It didn't fly too well. I think I know what I did wrong, though. I put all this fancy junk on it to make it look cool, and it got too heavy."

"Want to work on it this Saturday?" I asked.

For the first time that afternoon, Josh gave me a real, true Josh Rocker smile. "Sounds good," he replied.

I suddenly felt much more relaxed. Things between us now seemed normal. Maybe he'd just been in a mood. Everyone is entitled to a mood once in awhile.

Without talking, we watched the kites fly. There's something hypnotic about the way they sail in the sky, dipping and circling. At one point, the wind got hold of Josh's cap and he had to scramble down the rock to recover it.

As he climbed back up, cap in hand, I noticed a questioning expression in his eyes. He seemed about to say something. And then he did. "Claudia, do you think things between us are working out?"

"Sure," I replied quickly — maybe too quickly. The moment the words left my lips, I was hit with the unpleasant feeling that I'd just told a lie.

I hadn't meant to lie.

I didn't want to lie.

But that was how it *felt* — like a lie.

Josh smiled and seemed to accept my answer. But now I was upset over the question. I knew I loved Josh. He was so wonderful, how could I *not* love him?

But was I in love with him? Or did I love him as a friend? That was what I wasn't sure about.

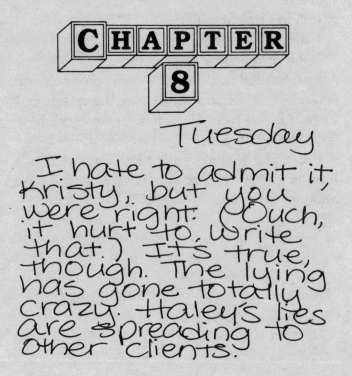

# CHAPTER 8

## Tuesday

I hate to admit it, Kristy, but you were right. (Ouch, it hurt to write that.) It's true, though. The lying has gone totally crazy. Haley's lies are spreading to other clients.

Abby wasn't the only one who couldn't believe it. But she was the first to hear it when she arrived at the GSBA basketball practice at the elementary school that afternoon.

She'd stepped into the supply closet to get the basketball. Some of the girls, including Haley, didn't see her there by the open door as they gathered just outside.

"It's true," Abby heard Haley say to the others. "She tells my parents everything. And guess what I found out. All of them do. They're spies for our parents."

"What do you mean?" Charlotte Johanssen asked.

"Just what I said," Haley went on knowingly. "If you tell them anything, they report it to our parents. If you do anything, they tell. I wouldn't even be surprised if they look through our things after we're asleep."

"That's a lie," Karen Brewer spoke up. "Kristy would never search through someone's private stuff."

"Neither would Jessi," Becca Ramsey said.

"All right, maybe they don't do that," Haley conceded. "But I know they tell on us. Look at what happened to me. That's proof."

"Hey, hey," Abby said, walking out of the supply closet. "Did I hear someone say the BSC is a bunch of spies?" Leave it to Abby to get right to the point. She's like that.

Haley went pale. The others looked guilty too.

But Haley quickly recovered. "Oh, no," she said with a phony little laugh. "I didn't say the BSC members were spies. I said, 'Did you see the spies?' There was a TV special on spies last night. It was very cool. Did you see it?"

Haley wasn't fooling Abby. "Are you sure that's what you said?" she challenged her.

Haley was a cool customer. "I know what I said," she replied.

Abby looked to the other girls to help her out, but they were all busy staring down at their feet or up at the ceiling. Even Karen examined her fingernails and wouldn't provide any assistance.

Becca was the only one who met her eyes. For a moment, Abby thought she might say something — maybe tell the truth about what Haley had said — but she kept her mouth closed.

Abby couldn't really blame her. No one wants to snitch on a friend.

She tossed the ball to Haley. "Come on, let's play basketball," she said, ending the awkward moment.

As they played, Abby stood on the sideline

with Kristy and told her what she'd heard Haley say.

"That's crazy. The other girls didn't believe it, did they?" Kristy asked with a scornful laugh.

"Karen and Becca tried to defend us," Abby replied. "But I couldn't tell about the others. They might have believed it."

"No way!" Kristy cried. "They know we're not spies. Just last week I patched up a big fight between Sara Hill and her brother, Norman. She was teasing him about his weight and he tripped her. I could have gotten them both in trouble but I didn't say a word about it."

Abby chuckled. "I suppose it didn't look too good — me bursting out of a closet and knowing every word they'd just said. It's the sort of thing a spy would do."

"You were getting the basketball!" Kristy cried. "You couldn't help overhearing! What are we supposed to do — pretend we don't have ears?"

Before Abby could reply, Kristy was blasting her whistle. She'd spotted Haley traveling with the ball.

"I did not travel!" Haley objected. "You're seeing things."

"Haley, if you back-talk a ref during a real

game, you're going to be sidelined and the team will be penalized," Kristy warned her sternly.

"Well, this isn't a real game. It's a practice, if you didn't notice," Haley shot back.

Abby watched red splotches of anger form on Kristy's face.

With a quick blast on her whistle, Kristy called a time-out. Then she walked back to Abby.

"Wow! I give you credit for not totally blowing your top," Abby commended her.

For a moment, Kristy looked as if she was almost too furious to speak. But when she did, it was in a remarkably calm voice. "If I hadn't walked away, I would have lost it for sure. What is with Haley these days?" she wondered out loud.

Abby shrugged and shook her head. "It's as if she thinks she can control everything by lying."

"If this keeps up," Kristy said, "I'm going to have to talk to Mrs. Braddock about Haley's behavior."

Over Kristy's shoulder, Abby suddenly noticed that Haley, Vanessa, Charlotte, Sara, and Becca stood in a group. They were close enough to hear what Kristy had just said.

With a confident grin, Haley nodded to her friends. Her smug expression spoke louder than words could. It said, *See? I told you so.* The other girls looked at Kristy with raised eyebrows.

"Don't look now," Abby said quietly to Kristy, "but Haley and some of the others just heard you say you were going to tell on Haley."

Kristy whirled around and looked at the girls. They scattered in all directions. "Oh, great, now they're afraid of me."

Abby laughed. "That's nothing. *I'm* afraid of you sometimes."

"Very funny," Kristy shot back with a grin. She blew her whistle and resumed the game.

By the time the game had ended, the weather had turned rainy and windy. Abby was nearly drenched by the time she arrived at her job sitting for the three Rodowsky boys. Shea is nine, Jackie is seven, and Archie is four. They are carrottops with freckles and lively personalities. Abby usually enjoys sitting for them.

But this afternoon, as she stood in the downstairs bathroom changing into the dry sweatshirt Mrs. Rodowsky had loaned her, she couldn't get over the feeling that something wasn't right.

For one thing, Shea and Jackie had said hello, then gone up to their rooms. When she stepped out of the bathroom, only little Archie was downstairs waiting for her. Usually all the boys liked to stay and talk.

"What are your brothers up to?" Abby asked Archie as she dried her hair with a bathroom towel.

"They're hiding from you," he told her.

"Hiding? Why?"

" 'Cause you're a spy."

"Oh, I am, huh? Then why aren't you hiding from me?"

Archie smiled. "I wanted to spy with you." He ran to the couch and took out a pair of green plastic binoculars he'd hidden under a throw pillow. "Want to spy on Noah Seger next door? He's playing in the yard in the rain."

"Archie!" Abby said, trying not to laugh. "I don't want to tell on Noah. Where did you get the idea I was a spy?"

"Shea said a girl in school told him."

"Was her name Haley by any chance?"

Archie nodded enthusiastically. "I think so. She said all the baby-sitters are spies. Do you work for the FZ-Guy?"

"Who?"

"The FZ-Guy!" Archie insisted, as if she should have known who that was.

"Do you mean the FBI?" Abby asked.

"No, I don't think so," Archie insisted. "The

FZ-Guy is a real superhero who catches bad guys."

"Well, I don't know him," she said, pretty sure he *did* mean the FBI, whether he knew it or not. "So I definitely don't work for him."

"Too bad," Archie said with a pout.

"Come on, let's go see what your brothers are doing," Abby suggested. When they reached the second floor, Shea's and Jackie's doors were both tightly closed.

She knocked on Shea's door first. No answer. "It's Abby. I know you're in there. I just want to talk to you."

The door opened a crack. "Hi," Shea said quietly. "What's up?"

"What's up with you?" Abby demanded. "Archie says you guys are hiding from me because you think I'm a spy."

Shea made a disgruntled face at Archie. "You won't tell my parents we were hiding, will you?" he asked.

"Of course not. But this is so silly. Why are you hiding? Are you doing something you shouldn't be doing?"

Before Shea could reply, Jackie came tumbling out through his bedroom doorway onto the floor. He looked up at them, red-faced with embarrassment.

Abby bit down on her laughter. It was easy to see what had happened. Jackie had been leaning on his door, trying to hear what was being said. He'd leaned too hard and the door had swung open. "And you guys think *I'm* a spy?" she said, smiling. "I don't go around listening to conversations behind closed doors."

Jackie turned an even deeper red.

Turning back to Shea, Abby noticed a splotch of cobalt-blue paint on his hand. "Okay, what are you doing in there?" she asked.

"Promise you won't tell?" Shea replied.

"No, I don't promise," Abby said. "Believe it or not, I don't tell your parents things you do wrong unless they really need to know. But I'm not promising anything. It depends on what you're doing."

Shea opened the door wider and revealed a half-painted model airplane on the floor. He'd put newspapers under it to protect the rug from the paint. "It's nice," Abby commented as she walked into the room. "What's wrong with doing this?"

"He's not supposed to do it in his room," Archie informed her.

"Why not?" Abby asked.

"Mom says she doesn't want me breathing in the glue so I always have to work on it outside," Shea explained. "And now that I'm at the painting part, she doesn't want the paint all over."

"Then you shouldn't be doing it," Abby pointed out.

"But I told my teacher I'd bring it to school tomorrow. It's an authentic model of a World War Two fighter plane. And we're learning about World War Two. I can't work outside today," he said, pointing toward the rain-splashed window. "You're going to tell, aren't you."

"No!" Abby cried impatiently. "The baby-sitters are not spies. Get that through your heads." She looked out the window, then down at the plane. "Why not work in the garage?"

"Okay," Shea agreed.

So Abby, Archie, and Jackie stood out in the garage and watched the rain fall while Shea sat on the garage floor and worked on his model.

After awhile, Abby needed to break the boredom. "Bet you can't catch me," she cried as she stepped out into the rain.

"Can so!" Archie shouted, running after her. Jackie followed, and even Shea took a break from his work to join the game of rain tag.

By the time Mrs. Rodowsky came home, the boys had changed into dry clothes and were inside watching TV. "I saw your model drying in the garage," she told Shea. "It looks great. Thanks for working in the garage."

"No problem," Shea replied, looking sideways at Abby.

She just winked at him and smiled.

# CHAPTER 9

"We have to do something about this — and right away," Kristy said at our Wednesday meeting. I'd rarely seen her so agitated. She was so worked up that she couldn't even sit still in the director's chair. She was pacing around my room, pounding one hand into the other. "Haley has got to be stopped," she insisted.

"That's the truth," said Jessi. "Last night Becca came into my room, sat down on the bed, and demanded an explanation. She wanted to know if I was a spy. My own sister!"

"Unbelievable!" Mary Anne cried softly.

Jessi nodded. "She said that at first she didn't believe it, but then she started thinking. She began wondering how my mom knew she was spending her lunch money on cookies instead of lunch. She asked, 'Did you tell her?' "

"That's so silly," Stacey said. "How would

you know what she's doing all the way over in the elementary school?"

"I know!" Jessi replied. "It was totally stupid. I told her, 'Mom knew because Aunt Cecelia told her you were coming home starving every day. Plus, she saw all the leftover change in your backpack.' " (Jessi's aunt Cecelia lives with them and minds the kids while Mr. and Mrs. Ramsey are at work.)

"If Becca suspects you — her own sister — what are the other kids thinking?" Kristy said.

"Charlotte Johanssen wouldn't let me see what she was writing today when I sat for her," Stacey reported.

"Was it her diary?" Mary Anne asked.

"No, it was only a composition for school. She said she wasn't sure she could trust me."

"But Charlotte *adores* you," I said.

"I know," Stacey agreed. "She even used to show me her diary sometimes. We're so close. I'd hate to lose that."

"I'm going over to the Braddocks' right after this meeting," Kristy said fiercely. "I'm going to talk to Little Miss Haley myself."

"I don't know if that's a good idea," Mary Anne cautioned her. "You're pretty worked up right now."

I agreed. "Listen, you don't have to go. I have a sitting job with them after the meeting. I'll talk to her."

"She won't listen to you," Kristy objected. "You're her main target."

"Just let me try. Maybe she has some problem with me and I need to be the one to straighten it out."

"I doubt it," Kristy said. "She's got some problem with herself — and she needs to straighten it out herself."

"Whatever," I said with a sigh. "But if we both go over there, she'll feel like we're ganging up on her. And if you go over while her parents are there, she'll just tell the world you told on her to her parents."

"I guess you're right," Kristy admitted, finally sinking into the director's chair. "Call me, though, if you need some backup. I'll be home."

"Thanks," I told her. "But things won't get that bad."

As I walked up the path to the Braddocks' house, I gave myself a little lecture. *Be pleasant. Don't go in there and confront Haley right away. Act normal. Pretend this is the old Haley, the one you liked before this little liar pod took over her body.*

I'd try to relate to the real Haley who was still trapped somewhere inside this alien life-form she'd become. (Okay. Maybe it was a little silly. But it was better than thinking Haley had changed forever.)

"Hi, Claudia," Mrs. Braddock greeted me at the door. "Come on in." She explained where she and Mr. Braddock would be, and that the kids had already eaten dinner. "Haley isn't grounded anymore," she said (which I already knew since I'd been told about the basketball practice). "The No TV Until Homework Rule still applies. And I want to know if she gives you any trouble at all."

Instead of saying "Sure" I hesitated. Then I said, "I don't think we'll have any trouble."

"Anything at all," Mrs. Braddock insisted. "I'm going, kids," she called. She blew Matt a kiss and left.

He signed a hi to me and smiled. I was glad he was still happy to see me.

He picked up a math workbook and gestured to me. I knew enough sign language to figure out that he wanted me to help him. Believe me, I'm not the person to tutor anyone in math. But, remembering how much easier seventh grade had been for me, I figured I could certainly help a second-grader. I smiled and nodded, sitting on the couch.

Matt sat next to me and opened the book. He was supposed to add a column of several numbers. I could handle that. But we did have a problem: no pencil.

I mimed writing and he understood. He began searching drawers in the living room. I tried to help, but we couldn't locate a pencil.

As we searched, Haley came downstairs. "Hi, Haley. Have you got a pencil?" I asked. "Or do you know where one is?"

"There are pencils downstairs in the basement on the table," she told me in an uninterested way.

"Thanks," I said and headed for the basement. When I got there, no pencils were to be found. I met Haley in the kitchen and asked her about it.

"Oops, my mistake," she said. Her sarcastic tone told me right away that she knew all along there were no pencils there.

"Then why did you lie about it?" I asked, trying hard to keep my voice neutral.

She shrugged.

"Haley, what is with you these days?"

"It's just a pencil," she replied.

"It's not the pencil, it's the lie."

"I can't believe you're getting bent out of shape over a pencil," she said. She pulled open a junk drawer and handed me a pencil. "Here."

"Thank you."

As I walked out of the room I heard her mutter under her breath, "Get a life, Claudia."

I turned. "Did you say something, Haley?"

"No," she replied with a fake sweet smile. It was infuriating, but what could I do?

Matt was waiting for me on the couch. I

never thought I'd be glad to do even the simplest math, but I was. It gave me a reason to ignore Haley for awhile. And eventually Matt got the hang of how to do it on his own, which felt satisfying.

About forty minutes later, Matt and I were playing his new video game while Haley sat on the couch browsing through a nature magazine.

"Shouldn't you be doing your homework?" I asked her.

"This is part of it. I'm looking something up."

"Can I see your assignment sheet?" I asked, doubting her.

"I didn't get one today," she replied, looking back down at her magazine.

Suddenly, Matt hopped up and began signing quickly to Haley. She signed back to him, and then he replied in sign language.

"What's going on?" I asked.

"Matt almost forgot," Haley said. "He needs to make a poster for school, but he doesn't have any poster paints."

"I have some at my house," I said. "Maybe someone can drive them over here." But only Janine was at home.

I looked at Matt, who wore a distressed expression. What could I do for him? Then I had an idea. I phoned Stacey. "Hi, it's me," I said when she answered. "I'm sorry to bother you, but could you do me a big favor? Do you think your mom could drive you to my house so you could get some poster paints? They're under my bed. I have a whole box of them. Then would you bring them to the Braddocks' house? I wouldn't ask except that it's really important. Almost an emergency. Matt needs them for his homework."

"I'm in the middle of writing a report . . . but all right," Stacey agreed reluctantly. "I think Mom can do it. I'll be right there."

After I hung up, Matt seemed happy again and returned to his video game. In about twenty minutes the front bell rang. Matt jumped up and followed me to the door. Sure enough, it was Stacey with the paints.

"Thank you *so* much," I told her, taking the box.

"No problem." Then at the same time, we both noticed Matt's unhappy, confused expression. "What's the matter?" Stacey asked. "Didn't you want these?"

He shook his head, frowning.

I was confused. Had I misunderstood? No, I hadn't. I'd acted on the information I'd received from Haley.

"Thanks, Stacey," I said. "Now I'm supersorry to have bothered you. I'll find out what's going on."

"Good luck," Stacey said warily.

I took the paints inside, setting them by the door. I was in time to see Haley trying to sneak upstairs. "Haley, didn't you tell me Matt needed to make a poster?" I demanded.

"No, I said he needed you to call Nicky Pike. He almost forgot that Nicky said he has a book on lizards Matt could borrow. He has to bring it in tomorrow as part of his group science project," she replied.

"That's not what you said!"

"Yes it is."

I couldn't believe what I was hearing. But I wasn't going to let it go. Not this time.

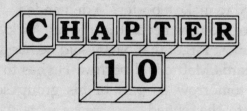

# CHAPTER 10

Haley," I said, "you stopped Stacey from writing her report, and made her mother drive her all the way to my house, and then here." My voice rose angrily. "All this time Matt's been waiting for Nicky to bring over the lizard book because he thought I called him. Now it's late. Your parents are going to have to get it when they come in. I don't understand. Why did you do it?"

"You're crazy, Claudia," Haley replied coolly. "I told you Matt needed a book from Nicky and he wanted you to remind him to bring it over."

Haley was really good at this. Her lie was close enough to the truth to give me a moment of doubt. Had I heard her wrong? No. I was sure I hadn't.

Matt tugged at the hem of my shirt. On a card he'd written the name Nicky Pike. I didn't want to let Haley get away, but I had to be fair to Matt. I made a gesture, as if I were talking on the phone, and went to the kitchen to call Nicky. Mrs. Pike answered. She didn't know what book I meant, and Mr. Pike had taken Nicky and the other kids to a movie. She'd ask him to call when they returned.

I did my best to explain this to Matt. A look of disappointment swept across his face and I felt terrible. He punched a fist into the palm of his other hand. Although he sometimes has difficulty communicating, at that moment I understood him loud and clear. He was totally frustrated with the confusion of having been misunderstood.

Not exactly misunderstood, though. Haley had understood him perfectly. I was pretty sure of that. She'd just chosen to lie to me again.

I charged back into the living room and found Haley on the couch again with her magazine. I took it from her hands. "Give that back!" she shouted, jumping to her feet.

"Not until you tell me why you're acting this way," I demanded.

"I'm not acting any way!"

The sound of jangling keys distracted us all. We turned toward Mr. and Mrs. Braddock, who'd come in together. They looked from Matt to Haley to me with darting eyes.

"It wasn't my fault," Haley blurted out, not even waiting to be blamed. "Claudia invited

81

Stacey over so they could hang out and she forgot to call Nicky about the lizard book like I told her Matt asked her to. Matt got upset. And Claudia said that if I didn't cover up for her, she'd tell you I'd lied to her and then I'd get into trouble."

My jaw dropped. I had to hand it to her — she was a fast thinker. I couldn't have thought up a lie that fast, even if I'd wanted to.

"That . . . that's not true," I said, stunned. I then explained what had actually happened. As I talked, I worried that Mr. and Mrs. Braddock might not believe me. They were still standing by the door, their coats on, wearing serious but unreadable expressions.

I also realized that there I was, telling on Haley. Right in front of her. The scene was playing beautifully into Haley's view of things. Me, the BSC spy, reporting on her.

I couldn't let her get away with this, though. She'd maneuvered me into a terrible position.

Mrs. Braddock took off her coat and hung it up. "Claudia, can I talk to you privately in the kitchen?" she requested.

My heart fluttered with anxiety. Did this mean she didn't believe me? That she believed Haley? It would be so embarrassing if she did. Embarrassing and unfair and depressing.

Mrs. Braddock would call the other BSC

clients. None of them would want me again as a sitter. They might even stop using the BSC altogether. All because of Haley's lie . . .

Mrs. Braddock pulled out a chair for herself and I did the same. My heart was pounding. Why did we have to talk privately?

"First, let me say that I don't believe Haley's story for a minute," she began.

What a relief! My heart slowed to normal.

"Her father and I don't know what's going on with her," Mrs. Braddock continued. "Maybe it's some surge of preadolescent rebellion, although she seems pretty young for that. We're completely bewildered, frankly. But it does seem — for whatever reason — that she behaves her worst when you're around. We have no idea why."

"I don't either," I said. "She and I used to get along great."

"I know you did. And I know that you're a good-hearted and trustworthy sitter. But my husband and I were discussing this on the way home, and we think it might be best if we use another sitter for the time being."

I knew she was trying to be as nice as she possibly could. Still, her words hurt.

For whatever reason, the Braddocks didn't want me to sit for their kids anymore. I was being pushed away. Fired. Rejected.

In my logical mind, I could understand their

reasoning. I even knew I wasn't being blamed for Haley's lies.

But inside, it just felt so wrong. Not only that, if I didn't see Haley anymore, I'd never straighten out the problem between us. What had happened to the person Haley used to be?

As I pushed back the kitchen chair and stood up, a scary thought came to me: What if that Haley was gone forever?

# CHAPTER 11

The moment Mary Anne walked into our Friday BSC meeting, I knew her sitting job at the Braddocks' hadn't gone well. "What happened?" I asked.

She was the last to arrive. Everyone else was waiting to hear her report.

Mary Anne sat on the edge of my bed and sighed. "Well, Haley firmly believes that we're all out to get her," she began. "She barely spoke to me the whole time I was there."

"Why was she angry at *you*?" I asked.

"I told you, it's all of us, though she's angriest at you because she thinks it's your fault that she's grounded again."

"It's her own fault!" I cried, once again feeling the injustice of it all.

"We know that," Kristy said. "But she obviously doesn't."

"You're not her only target, Claudia," Mary Anne added. "She told me a couple of lies while I was there. When I wanted to make a call, she said the phone wasn't working because her parents couldn't afford to pay the bill and probably wouldn't be able to pay me either. Then, the next minute, I heard her chatting away to Vanessa."

"She didn't want you to use the phone so she could use it first," Abby surmised, shaking her head in grim amazement at Haley's nerve.

"Right," Mary Anne agreed. "And later she blamed Matt for spilling some milk on the floor when she was the one who'd just left it there after it spilled."

"The girl is totally out of control," Kristy commented.

"She sure is," Jessi agreed. "Today Becca told me she's saying we send weekly reports to the teachers of the kids we sit for."

"She really said that?!" Stacey cried in disbelief.

Jessi nodded. "She's saying we tell the teachers if they've copied a report from the encyclopedia or another book. She's told kids that we let their teachers know if they say something insulting about him or her."

"That is too weird," Abby remarked.

"You know," I said, "it's as if all this lying began with that *Great Brain* report."

"Mrs. Braddock said she'd lied about homework before that," Stacey reminded me.

"That's true," I agreed. "But Haley wasn't lying to us — or *about* us — before then. I wish I could somehow get back to that moment and change something."

"There's nothing you could have done differently," Abby pointed out.

"Maybe not, but it might give me a better idea of what was going on in Haley's head at the time."

"Well, you can't go back," Kristy said.

"Wait, maybe you can," said Mary Anne. "When I was in counseling, we did something called role-playing."

Awhile ago, Mary Anne was having difficulty understanding some of her feelings. So she saw a psychologist. Now she knows all this great stuff about emotions and dealing with them.

"When you role-play you act out different parts and replay a moment from your life," Mary Anne explained. "I wonder how the Braddocks would feel if we did that with Haley."

Kristy picked up the phone. "Let's find out," she suggested as she dialed the Braddocks' number. Mrs. Braddock picked up. (Which was probably a good thing. If Haley had received a call from Kristy asking to speak to Mrs. Braddock, you can imagine what she would have told the kids at school.)

Kristy gave the phone to Mary Anne and let her explain the plan. Mary Anne listened, nodding, while Mrs. Braddock spoke. "Great," Mary Anne said. "We'll be there tomorrow."

When she hung up, her eyes were bright with excitement. "Okay, we're on for tomorrow at twelve-thirty. We're going to meet with Mr. and Mrs. Braddock first. Then Haley will come home from basketball practice and we'll do it."

"I sure hope it works," Kristy said. "I'd hate to have to drop the Braddocks from our client list."

"They might drop us first," I added. "I've already been dropped."

Kristy nodded, looking worried. "If Haley's lies spread, a lot of our customers could start dropping us."

A week or so ago we'd have told her not to worry so much. But now we were quiet. Who knew how much further it would go if we weren't able to stop Haley?

The phone rang then. Mrs. Rodowsky wanted a sitter for the next night. After Stacey took that job, Mrs. Newton called needing a sitter. We were busy with client calls right up until six o'clock. We even took a 6:05 call from Mr. Brooke, who always phones either right before or after our meetings and drives us crazy.

Soon my room was empty except for Stacey, who'd stayed behind to hang out before going home. "This role-playing thing makes me nervous," she said, flopping down onto my bed. "What if Haley doesn't go for it?"

"We won't be any worse off than we are now," I said as I sat in my director's chair.

"True."

"It makes me uneasy too," I admitted. I hate confrontations. Usually I'll do anything to avoid one.

"Not to change the subject from Haley . . ." Stacey began.

"Oh, please do."

Stacey smiled. "Okay. I'm going into Manhattan on Sunday to see Dad and Ethan. I was thinking it might be fun if you and Josh came with me. The four of us could do something together during the day." I sighed. "What's the problem? Don't you want to? I know Josh is intimidated by Ethan because of their age difference. Is that it?"

"No," I told her. "But the problem *is* Josh."

Stacey sat cross-legged on the bed. "What? I thought everything was great between the two of you."

"*Josh* is great. But I don't know how great everything is *between* us."

"What's wrong?"

Suddenly I felt embarrassed. Stacey is my best friend and I tell her *everything*. Somehow, though, this was hard to talk about.

"What?" she asked again.

"Like I said, it's nothing against Josh," I began. "I mean, he's adorable, he's sweet, he's funny. He's even a great kisser. The problem is with me, really."

"*What's* the problem?"

"I don't want to kiss him," I blurted out. "It's strange, I know. I just never feel the desire to kiss him and when I think he's going to kiss me, I duck out of it. Though, come to think of it, he hasn't even tried to kiss me in awhile."

"What's awhile?"

"A week or so," I figured, thinking back. "We get along great. It's just this kissing thing. Do you think it's a problem?"

"Sort of," Stacey said. "It sounds to me like your romance is turning into a friendship."

Stacey is so smart sometimes. That was *exactly* what was happening, though I hadn't realized it until she'd said it. Josh and I had started as friends. We'd had a romance, but it was returning to what it had been in the beginning — a friendship.

"That's it!" I cried. "You've figured it out." Then I slumped lower in the chair. "How am I going to tell this to Josh?"

"Tell him just what you told me," Stacey suggested.

"Yeah," I said glumly. "The old 'let's just be friends' talk. You know guys always take that

90

as a brush-off. Girls do too, I suppose. It sounds like a put-down."

"But it's not," Stacey replied. "You don't mean it that way. You really believe that you two were meant to be friends, not boyfriend and girlfriend."

"I know. I think a friend is just as important as a boyfriend. It might even be more important because friends usually last a lot longer than most boyfriends. It just sounds so awful to the person who has to hear it."

"I know," Stacey admitted. "And it isn't easy to stay friends with a guy after you've dated him. Robert and I weren't really friends again for a long time after we broke up."

"You're friends now, though," I said hopefully.

"True, but it wasn't easy."

As we talked, I realized I wasn't one bit upset at the thought of losing Josh as a boyfriend. The idea of losing him as a friend panicked me, though. "If it means losing his friendship, then I'd rather not say anything to him," I told Stacey.

"You can't do that. For one thing, you'll be miserable. For another, it's not exactly fair to him, or honest. When are you going to tell him?"

"We're going to the movies tonight."

"So tell him tonight."

"I can't," I wailed. It was too hard. I just couldn't.

"You have to. It's the truth."

"I know."

But I really, really wished I didn't have to do what I was about to do.

# CHAPTER 12

"Hi, Claudia. You look nice," Josh said that evening when he arrived at my house.

My mother came into the hall and greeted him. "Hello, Josh. It's good to see you."

Josh shifted from foot to foot. "Thank you. It's good to see you too."

"You're going to a seven o'clock show?" she asked.

"Yes," he replied.

"Don't worry, I can be home by ten. Easy," I assured Mom. I didn't want to say what I was thinking — that I might be home by *eight*, depending on whether I had my talk with Josh before or after the movie.

Mr. Rocker drove us out to Washington Mall and dropped us off in the parking lot. I checked my watch. "We're a little early," I said. "What do you want to do?"

"I don't know. Do you want to get something to eat?"

I wasn't hungry, but it was something to kill time. "Sure. How about Friendly's?"

He agreed and we set off. I wasn't surprised that I didn't have much to say. I'd decided to talk to Josh after the movie. I figured that by then his father would be on his way to pick us up and — in case the talk didn't go well — at least we'd be heading home instead of stuck at the mall together for hours.

Again and again, I mentally rehearsed what I would say to Josh, changing this part, taking out another, adding something new.

What surprised me, though, was Josh. He didn't seem to have anything to say either.

We walked into Friendly's and slid into a booth. We both ordered french fries and sodas. "Claudia, we have to talk," Josh said after the waitress left.

"Yes, we do," I agreed eagerly. Relief flooded me. He thought we had to talk too. He was aware that something was wrong. It wasn't only me.

"You go first," we both said at the same time, which made us laugh.

"No, you," I insisted.

"Okay." Josh took a deep breath. "Things between us are getting . . . strange." He spoke slowly, picking each word carefully. "Sometimes I feel more like your younger brother than your boyfriend."

94

Unbelievable! He was saying just what I felt. I did think of him more as a younger brother than a boyfriend. It explained why I didn't want to kiss him.

"I know what you mean," I said.

He frowned. "You do? . . . I mean . . . is that how you think of me?"

"Sometimes," I blurted out. "I mean, I think you're great. I couldn't care about you or like you more than I do. But I think of you as a brother . . . or a friend."

"A friend," he repeated.

"Does that hurt your feelings?"

He sat back in the booth and looked at me with troubled eyes. It seemed like a very long time before he spoke again.

"I was going to say that it did hurt my feelings. . . . I had the idea that it *should* upset me. Only, it doesn't."

"Really?"

"I think I feel the same way about you," he said.

To my surprise, his words hurt *my* feelings. It was like a blow to my pride. But the pain lasted for only a second. Then the hurt was replaced by a quiet happiness. This wasn't going to be so terrible after all.

"I guess this means we're breaking up," he said sadly.

"As boyfriend and girlfriend we are, but not

as friends," I replied. "Do you think that's possible?"

He pressed his fingers together and seemed to consider the question. As I waited for his answer, I remembered that I was no longer friends with my old boyfriend Mark. And that so few people I knew were able to remain friends after breaking up. Still, I liked to think that Josh and I weren't like other people. Our relationship went pretty deep.

"We won't know until we try," he answered at last.

That was good enough for me. Smiling, I reached across the table and took hold of his hand. "I think we can. It's worth it to me to try."

He smiled back at me. "Me too."

The waitress arrived with our food. It tasted a lot better than it would have if I'd had to sit there and eat it while I worried about talking to Josh.

I felt light and free and happy. Josh obviously felt better too. The quiet between us lifted.

We went to the movie soon after. Josh didn't hold my hand, and I didn't worry about it too much. We were friends now. We could relax.

When the movie ended, an unhappy thought came to me. Now that Josh and I were friends, how would we see each other? Could we just call each other like we used to and arrange to do things together? I wasn't sure.

But — as often happened — Josh was thinking the same thing. "Why don't we go out on a friendship date this Sunday afternoon," he suggested. "It will show that we really can be friends."

"We talked about kite flying tomorrow," I reminded him.

"I don't know," he replied thoughtfully. "Tomorrow might be a little *too* soon."

Josh's dad met us and drove us home. As Josh always did, he walked me to the door of my house.

"Well," he said uneasily. "This is our last night as boyfriend and girlfriend. But I'll see you Sunday as pals."

"Yeah," I replied. "See you Sunday."

I leaned in for one last good-night kiss. In a second, I saw he'd extended his hand. I quickly stuck out my hand. He changed his mind too and leaned in for a kiss.

We both laughed uncomfortably. This change wasn't going to be easy.

"Well, good night," I said.

" 'Night," Josh replied, walking backward down the front path. He tripped slightly but kept going.

Oh, well . . . at least it was a start.

# CHAPTER 13

"This is totally dumb and I'm not doing it!" Haley folded her arms and turned away from us.

Somehow I wasn't surprised by Haley's reaction to our role-playing plan. I gazed around the Braddocks' living room at Stacey, Mary Anne, and Mr. and Mrs. Braddock, hoping that one of them had a clue as to what to do next. Luckily, Mrs. Braddock took charge. "Haley, do you want to be grounded for more time or less time?" she asked.

"Less, of course," Haley grumbled, not looking at her mother.

"If you do this, we'll cut time from your punishment," Mrs. Braddock told her calmly. "If you refuse, we'll add more time."

Haley faced her angrily. "In other words, you're making me do this."

"No, it's your choice," Mr. Braddock said.

"Some choice," Haley muttered. "Let's get this over with."

"All right," Mary Anne jumped in. "Why don't we start with Haley playing the part of herself and Claudia being herself? Stacey, you be Mrs. Braddock."

"I can't believe this," Haley muttered.

Stacey began. "Make sure Haley doesn't watch TV until her homework is done," she said as she stood by the front door.

"All right," I agreed.

Stacey opened and shut the front door, pretending to leave. Then I turned toward Haley. "Better get your homework done, Haley."

Haley's hand flew to her hips. "That is not how you said it," she objected. "It was more like, 'Haley! Do your homework. Now!' Then I asked, 'Claudia, may I call Vanessa for a brief check on our homework?' You said, 'No, you may not. *I* want to chat with Vanessa. You do your work!' "

"Haley!" I cried. "That is just not true."

"You can't play both parts," Mary Anne told Haley. "Let's try it again."

We did it again. This time Haley didn't stop me. She presented herself as speaking to Vanessa for the briefest second.

"Wait a minute." Mr. Braddock stopped us. "If you were on and off the phone that fast, when did Claudia have time to get on the other extension? The way you show it, you were off before she could even have walked upstairs."

"Okay, so I talked a little longer than that," Haley admitted sullenly.

"After the call, you were up in your room," Mary Anne said. "What were you doing up there?"

"Homework," Haley replied.

"If you were doing homework, then why did you show me last month's report?" I asked. "Why didn't you bring me the right one?"

Tears sprang to Haley's eyes. "Because I hadn't finished the book!" she shouted as tears streamed down her face. "It was too hard and I didn't understand what it was trying to say!" Crying hard, she pushed past me and ran up the stairs.

"Haley!" Mrs. Braddock called, but Haley didn't stop.

That's when it came to me — an idea about what had happened to Haley.

"Can I go talk to her?" I asked the Braddocks.

Mr. and Mrs. Braddock looked at each other. "All right," Mrs. Braddock said.

I hurried up the stairs and into Haley's room. She sat on her bed, sobbing into her hands. "What's freaking you out about school?" I asked as soon as I stepped through the doorway.

"Everything!" she shouted tearfully. "I can't do the work. I didn't used to be stupid, but this year I am. I don't know why."

"You're not stupid!" I said. But I sure knew how she felt. Once schoolwork starts to get the better of you, it feels as if you'll never get it under control again. I had certainly experienced that feeling . . . many times.

Haley turned away from me. "You don't know how it is, Claudia."

I laughed. "Don't I? Schoolwork is the biggest problem I have in my entire life. I struggle with it all the time. Haley, they put me back a grade for awhile."

That caught her attention. She turned to me. "They did?"

"Yes."

"Wow," she said. "Didn't you hate that?"

"At first. But it turned out to be a good thing. It helped me get back on track with school."

Haley wiped her eyes with the back of her hand. "We're reading this book, *A Wrinkle in Time*, in school. Everyone else in the class thinks it's so great. But I don't have any idea what's going on."

"Maybe you should ask someone to explain it to you," I suggested.

She shook her head. "They'd know I was dumb then."

"Even Vanessa?" I asked.

"She's a brain. I don't want her to know."

"Is it just this one book that's giving you trouble?"

"No," Haley replied. "We're doing fractions, which make no sense to me. How can two thirds be the same as four sixths? Does that make any sense?"

It hadn't made sense to me in fourth grade either, although I understood the idea behind equivalent fractions now. (Probably because Stacey had explained it to me about a thousand times.)

Mr. Braddock came to the door. He knocked and walked in. "How's it going in here?"

I was about to say, "The problem turns out to be schoolwork," but I caught myself just in time. I didn't want to seem like a snitch again.

"Did I hear something about school?" Mr. Braddock asked.

Haley nodded and told him what she'd told me, only more calmly. Her father listened, then nodded. "When I was in fourth grade I was so bad at multiplication that I had the times tables written up my arms, on my ankles, on my elbows. My parents wondered why I never wanted to take a bath. It was because then I'd have to rewrite all those equations again. But you know what? After every bath, I became a little better at multiplication."

That set Haley off into gales of laughter. "Dad, you are so strange," she said.

"It's true," he insisted, laughing too. "Every time I rewrote those tables, I learned them a little better."

"Maybe I should try that with fractions," Haley said. "It's easier than lying."

"How did the lying get started?" Mr. Braddock asked. I was glad he got to the point. It still wasn't clear to me exactly how the lying fit into the school problem.

"Well," Haley began, "I lied to my teacher about why I didn't have my homework and she believed me. All day I was worried about getting into trouble, but then it didn't happen because I told a lie. Lying suddenly seemed like a pretty good idea."

"So then you tried it again with me?" I guessed.

Haley nodded. "It didn't work that time. But I lied the next day in school about why I didn't have the report — I said the computer conked out — and I got away with it again."

"So that made it seem like a solution to all your problems?" Mr. Braddock asked.

"In a way," Haley agreed. "It seemed like everything could be solved by lying."

I saw how it all fit together. Haley had been

mad at me, so she saw a way to get instant re-venge — by lying. Lying must have made her feel powerful.

Mrs. Braddock came in. Her husband turned to her. "I think we need to get Haley some tu-toring so she doesn't have to resort to lying as the ultimate secret weapon."

"Is that what's been happening?" Mrs. Brad-dock asked. Haley nodded. Mrs. Braddock sat beside her daughter and put her arm around her. "That doesn't excuse it, though," she said gently. "You know what you've been doing is wrong, don't you?"

"Sorry," Haley muttered.

"And perhaps you owe Claudia an apology," Mrs. Braddock added.

"Oh, it's okay," I jumped in.

Mrs. Braddock put her hand up to stop me. "Haley," she prompted.

"Sorry, Claudia," Haley said.

"No problem." I accepted Haley's apology, but I wasn't sure if she was sincere or simply doing the easiest thing at the moment. I wanted to believe she meant it. I hoped the ly-ing alien life-form that had taken her over was now winging its way back to its home planet.

But only time would tell if Haley was ready to start being honest again.

# CHAPTER 14

Sunday.

Our first GSBA scrimmage. Major excitement. We got to test ourselves as a team for the first time against the Franklin Township team. As coach, I worried that I hadn't worked the girls hard enough. And when Haley arrived I wasn't sure whether I was glad to see her.

P.S. Claudia, what's with the blue waistbands on the uniforms?

Kristy was incredibly excited about the scrimmage. She was in constant motion. "Their team is kind of short," she said to Stacey as she checked out Franklin Township on the far side of the gym. "Don't you think our girls are taller, mostly?"

Stacey nodded. "It looks that way."

Kristy frowned. "But if they're better players, height won't matter. The Franklin Township team might be fast and good with the ball. Sometimes short kids can really run."

"Don't worry so much," said Stacey. "It's just a game."

"But a game's no fun if you don't play to win."

The GSBA members were thrilled to be wearing their uniforms for the first time. But they didn't look exactly as Kristy had pictured them. (When she told me this, I just nodded and smiled.)

Kristy glanced into the bleachers and saw the Ramseys, her own parents, Dr. Johanssen, and several other parents she recognized. Someone tapped her on her shoulder and she turned.

"Hi," Haley said a little shyly.

"You're here!" Kristy hadn't been sure if Haley's punishment would be lifted in time for the game.

"Can I play?" Haley asked.

"I don't know. You haven't practiced as much as the other girls," Kristy replied. Still, she knew Haley was a pretty good player. "I'm not going to start you," she said after a moment's thought. "But if things are going well, I'll put you in."

"Okay," Haley agreed.

When it was time to begin, Kristy sent out her starting players. Vanessa jumped for the opening ball.

"Okay!" Kristy and Stacey shouted in unison as Vanessa took control of the basketball and steamed downcourt with it.

"Go, Vanessa, go!" Stacey screamed.

"Yesss!" Kristy cheered as, within seconds, Vanessa sunk the first basket of the game.

By the halfway mark, the GSBA had a six-point lead over Franklin Township. Kristy turned to Haley, who sat with several other teammates on folding chairs at the sideline. "Haley, you replace Becca. Charlotte, you replace Sara. And Karen, you take Diana's place." She wanted all the girls to play, and with a lead, she felt she could put in her second-string players.

She watched, anxiously chewing on her lower lip, as the second half of the game began.

"I'm not sure that was such a great idea," Kristy said to Stacey several minutes into the second half of the game. Franklin Township had taken control of the ball and kept it for the last three minutes, sinking two baskets. The GSBA was down to a two-point lead.

"It's more important that the girls get to play," Stacey remarked. "You did the right thing."

"Maybe," Kristy said, not sounding too certain. "Uh-oh," she said. She'd spotted Haley pushing into a Franklin Township girl while guarding her. The ref saw it at the same time and blasted her whistle.

Haley began arguing.

"I hope she's not trying to lie her way out of this," Stacey remarked.

"I'd better get out there," Kristy said as she hurried onto the court.

"I didn't touch her." Haley was disagreeing with the ref when Kristy arrived.

"I'm sorry, young lady, but I saw you," the ref replied.

Haley noticed Kristy, and their eyes met. Kristy couldn't believe it. After everything Haley had said the evening before, she was lying again.

Haley must have read Kristy's disappointed expression. "Maybe I did push her," she said. "I didn't mean to, but I might have accidentally nudged her."

Kristy smiled at her. Even though the foul

would cost the GSBA, it was more important that Haley had admitted the truth. She shot Haley a thumbs-up.

The free throws that the Franklin Township team won from Haley's foul tied up the score. Kristy called a time-out and rearranged the players again. "Want me to sit?" Haley asked.

Kristy shook her head. "No, you're playing well. Just be more careful while you're guarding. Stand back a little more."

"Okay. I'll try."

In the end, the GSBA won by two points. And it was Haley who sunk the winning basket. "Considering it was your first game as a team, you were excellent," Kristy congratulated them. "I saw some things we're going to work on. But mostly you girls rocked."

They cheered, pumping their fists in the air, and jumped up and down, hugging one another.

"I'll see you all at practice on Tuesday," she called to them as their group broke up and headed in various directions.

Haley ran toward her parents, who stood waiting by the door. Halfway there, she turned and hurried back toward Kristy and Stacey. "Did you forget something?" Kristy asked.

"Yeah," Haley said. "I forgot to say thanks for letting me play." She looked down at her hands. "I know I've been a pain lately. So . . . thanks."

Kristy punched her arm lightly. "No problem. Keep playing like you did today and I'll start you next time."

Haley smiled up at her. "I will." With a wave, she ran back toward her parents.

"Wow, the old Haley has returned," Stacey said.

"I know," Kristy agreed. "There may be hope for that kid yet."

# CHAPTER 15

On Sunday afternoon the weather was beautiful. It was windy, the kind of wind that makes your hair fly around like crazy. But it was warm and sunny — one of those days that lets you believe spring really will come soon.

Josh showed up at my house for our friendship date holding a khaki-green canvas bag. "What's that?" I asked as I opened the door and stepped out. "Kites?"

"Boats."

"Excuse me?"

He pulled open the drawstring mouth of the bag and I peered inside. "Are those toy sailboats?" I asked.

He nodded. "They were in my garage. I'd forgotten all about them. I was trying to find some old kites but I found these instead. I thought we could sail them in the pond at Miller's Park."

A blast of wind wrapped my hair around my

face. "Good idea," I said, from behind my hair. "It's sure windy enough."

Miller's Park is on the outskirts of Stoneybrook. It's a good twenty-five-minute walk from my house. We didn't mind, though.

For the first time in awhile, talk flowed easily between us. We chatted about school and people. I told him about my role-play with Haley the day before.

"That took guts," he commented. "A lot of kids couldn't deal with a confrontation like that. I bet some adults couldn't either."

"I was nervous," I admitted. "But facing it turned out to be the right thing."

"Just like with us," he commented.

I nodded, feeling awkward. "Yeah," I agreed.

We arrived at Miller's Park and walked along the rushing stream. On one bank stood an abandoned sawmill with a real waterwheel on the outside. In a patch of bright sun, I spotted a cluster of daffodils with fat buds just about to pop.

We followed the stream to a pond. "I never even knew this pond was here," I told Josh, although I'd been to the park a number of times.

"It's nice, isn't it? This pond must have an underground spring that feeds it and the stream," he said as he took the boats from the bag. Each was about two feet long and just as high. The one he handed me had two red sails, while his had three white ones.

We put the boats in the pond and watched as the wind filled their sails. Off they sped, tilting to one side as they went along.

"How are we going to get them back?" I asked.

"By keeping our fingers crossed," he replied.

"You're kidding."

"Sort of. They usually hit the shore eventually."

We spent the rest of the afternoon running along the edge of the pond like lunatics, trying to keep up with the boats.

I screamed, then laughed, then screamed again as my boat crashed into a patch of water reeds. "Oh, no!" I cried. "What do I do now?"

Josh picked up a long branch from the ground. "Try this," he suggested.

He gripped my wrist for support and I leaned far over the water with the branch in my hand, batting at the boat, trying to set it free.

"Whoa!" he shouted when I leaned too far, throwing us both off balance. Thinking fast, he grabbed the long branches of a nearby willow tree and steadied us. The motion of falling forward, then pulling back set my boat free, and we laughed as we watched it shoot off into the middle of the pond.

"Thank goodness," I said, laughing. "I didn't want to land in that water."

"I know," he agreed. "It's a nice day, but not *that* nice."

We stayed for more than two hours and had a great time. As Josh had predicted, the boats did eventually skirt along the edge of the pond, about three feet from us.

With long branches, we were able to pull them close enough so they could be plucked from the water.

"Ew, they're cold," I said, shaking the pond water from my hands.

"At least this day proves one thing," Josh said.

"What?"

"That our friendship is really going to work."

I looked at him and smiled. "I think you're right," I said, setting down my boat.

It seemed like the moment for a kiss. But that would have been out of place on a friendship date. Yet a handshake seemed wrong also. Way too formal.

Josh opened his arms and folded me into a hug. I hugged him back. We both held on tight.

And it felt absolutely, one hundred percent, perfectly right.

Dear Reader,

In *Claudia and the Little Liar*, Claudia and her friends
baby-sit for Haley, who's having a difficult time in
school and covers up by telling a lie. Before she knows
it, the lie snowballs, and Haley and the baby-sitters are
in big trouble. It's amazing how many problems one little lie can cause. Most of the time when we lie, we're trying to get ourselves out of trouble. But one lie often
leads to more lies and more trouble. A lie is often tempt-
ing to tell because it seems like the easy way out of a difficult situation. Haley's first lie seemed like a good idea
to her at the time — it seemed easier to tell a lie than to
confess she couldn't do her homework. But that one little lie led to another . . . then another . . . and another.

Almost everyone lies once in a while. But a good rule
of thumb is to remember that in the long run your lie is
going to cause more trouble than telling the truth, as difficult as the truth might seem. If Haley had only told the
truth and asked for help, she would have saved herself
and the BSC a lot of trouble!

Happy reading!

Ann M. Martin

Ann M. Martin

# About the Author

ANN MATTHEWS MARTIN was born on August 12, 1955. She grew up in Princeton, NJ, with her parents and her younger sister, Jane.

Although Ann used to be a teacher and then an editor of children's books, she's now a full-time writer. She gets ideas for her books from many different places. Some are based on personal experiences. Others are based on childhood memories and feelings. Many are written about contemporary problems or events.

All of Ann's characters, even the members of the Baby-sitters Club, are made up. (So is Stoneybrook.) But many of her characters are based on real people. Sometimes Ann names her characters after people she knows, other times she chooses names she likes.

In addition to the Baby-sitters Club books, Ann Martin has written many other books for children. Her favorite is *Ten Kids, No Pets* because she loves big families and she loves animals. Her favorite Baby-sitters Club book is *Kristy's Big Day*. (By the way, Kristy is her favorite baby-sitter!)

Ann M. Martin now lives in New York with her cats, Gussie, Woody, and Willy. Her hobbies are reading, sewing, and needlework — especially making clothes for children.

# Notebook Pages

This Baby-sitters Club book belongs to _____.

I am _____ years old and in the _____

grade.

The name of my school is _____.

I got this BSC book from _____.

I started reading it on _____ and

finished reading it on _____.

The place where I read most of this book is _____.

My favorite part was when _____.

If I could change anything in the story, it might be the part when

_____

My favorite character in the Baby-sitters Club is _____.

The BSC member I am most like is _____

because _____.

If I could write a Baby-sitters Club book it would be about _____

_____.

# #128 Claudia and the Little Liar

In *Claudia and the Little Liar*, Haley Braddock starts telling lies —
about Claudia. The biggest lie anyone has ever told about me was

_____

_____. The biggest lie I ever told

about someone else was _____

_____. Claudia herself lies

when she tells Josh that she's busy when she's not. Soon this little

lie becomes a big problem. Claudia wishes she had never told the

lie in the first place! One lie I wish I never told is _____

_____

_____. In the end, Claudia tells Josh the truth, and

feels much better. If my friend was deciding whether to lie to me

or tell me the truth about something, I would want him or her to

_____ because _____

_____. If I were

in the same situation, I would _____

_____.

# CLAUDIA'S

*Finger painting at 3...*

*A spooky sitting adventu*

*Sitting for two of my favorite charges --*
*Jamie and Lucy Newton.*

# SCRAPBOOK

...oil painting
at 13!

my family. Mom and Dad, me and
Janine... and we'll never forget Mimi.

Interior art by Angelo Tillery

Read all the books
about **Claudia**
in the Baby-sitters Club series
by Ann M. Martin

*Mysteries:*

*Portrait Collection:*

Look for #129

KRISTY AT BAT

Only one other person was standing by the bulletin board near the entrance to the gym. It was the tall blonde girl I'd seen at tryouts. "Hey!" I said, strolling up to her.

"Hi," she said a little shyly.

"Did you make the team?" I asked.

She nodded. "Second string," she said. I could tell she was disappointed.

I gave her an encouraging smile. "Excellent," I told her. "It's a great place to work on your skills."

She gave me a small smile in return.

"Let's see how I did," I said. I glanced up at the first-string list and ran my finger down it. Bummer. Coach Wu hadn't put me at first base.

Or second.

Or third.

In fact, I wasn't even in the outfield.

My name was not on the first-string list.

I raised my eyebrows. "Hmmm," I said. The blonde girl was still standing there. Suddenly, I felt hot all over. Then cold. What was happening here?

"Um — aren't you Kristy Thomas?" asked the girl.

I nodded.

She pointed to the middle of the second-string list. There, next to the words "Left Field," was my name.

It had to be a mistake.

Second string?

# THE BABY-SITTERS CLUB®

**Collect 'em all!**

## 100 (and more) Reasons to Stay Friends Forever!

*More titles...* ▸

## The Baby-sitters Club titles continued...

| | | | |
|---|---|---|---|
| ❑ MG22881-1 | #97 | Claudia and the World's Cutest Baby | $3.99 |
| ❑ MG22882-X | #98 | Dawn and Too Many Sitters | $3.99 |
| ❑ MG69205-4 | #99 | Stacey's Broken Heart | $3.99 |
| ❑ MG69206-2 | #100 | Kristy's Worst Idea | $3.99 |
| ❑ MG69207-0 | #101 | Claudia Kishi, Middle School Dropout | $3.99 |
| ❑ MG69208-9 | #102 | Mary Anne and the Little Princess | $3.99 |
| ❑ MG69209-7 | #103 | Happy Holidays, Jessi | $3.99 |
| ❑ MG69210-0 | #104 | Abby's Twin | $3.99 |
| ❑ MG69211-9 | #105 | Stacey the Math Whiz | $3.99 |
| ❑ MG69212-7 | #106 | Claudia, Queen of the Seventh Grade | $3.99 |
| ❑ MG69213-5 | #107 | Mind Your Own Business, Kristy! | $3.99 |
| ❑ MG69214-3 | #108 | Don't Give Up, Mallory | $3.99 |
| ❑ MG69215-1 | #109 | Mary Anne To the Rescue | $3.99 |
| ❑ MG05988-2 | #110 | Abby the Bad Sport | $3.99 |
| ❑ MG05989-0 | #111 | Stacey's Secret Friend | $3.99 |
| ❑ MG05990-4 | #112 | Kristy and the Sister War | $3.99 |
| ❑ MG05911-2 | #113 | Claudia Makes Up Her Mind | $3.99 |
| ❑ MG05911-2 | #114 | The Secret Life of Mary Anne Spier | $3.99 |
| ❑ MG05993-9 | #115 | Jessi's Big Break | $3.99 |
| ❑ MG05994-7 | #116 | Abby and the Worst Kid Ever | $3.99 |
| ❑ MG05995-5 | #117 | Claudia and the Terrible Truth | $3.99 |
| ❑ MG05996-3 | #118 | Kristy Thomas, Dog Trainer | $3.99 |
| ❑ MG05997-1 | #119 | Stacey's Ex-Boyfriend | $3.99 |
| ❑ MG05998-X | #120 | Mary Anne and the Playground Fight | $3.99 |
| ❑ MG50063-5 | #121 | Abby in Wonderland | $3.99 |
| ❑ MG50064-3 | #122 | Kristy in Charge | $3.99 |
| ❑ MG50174-7 | #123 | Claudia's Big Party | $3.99 |
| ❑ MG50175-5 | #124 | Stacey McGill...Matchmaker? | $3.99 |
| ❑ MG50179-8 | #125 | Mary Anne In the Middle | $3.99 |
| ❑ MG50349-9 | #126 | The All-New Mallory Pike | $4.50 |
| ❑ MG50350-2 | #127 | Abby's Un-Valentine | $4.50 |
| ❑ MG50351-0 | #128 | Claudia and the Little Liar | $4.50 |
| ❑ MG45575-3 | | Logan's Story Special Edition Readers' Request | $3.25 |
| ❑ MG47118-X | | Logan Bruno, Boy Baby-sitter | |
| | | Special Edition Readers' Request | $3.50 |
| ❑ MG47756-0 | | Shannon's Story Special Edition | $3.50 |
| ❑ MG47686-6 | | The Baby-sitters Club Guide to Baby-sitting | $3.25 |
| ❑ MG47314-X | | The Baby-sitters Club Trivia and Puzzle Fun Book | $2.50 |
| ❑ MG48400-1 | | BSC Portrait Collection: Claudia's Book | $3.50 |
| ❑ MG22864-1 | | BSC Portrait Collection: Dawn's Book | $3.50 |
| ❑ MG69181-3 | | BSC Portrait Collection: Kristy's Book | $3.99 |
| ❑ MG22865-X | | BSC Portrait Collection: Mary Anne's Book | $3.99 |
| ❑ MG48399-4 | | BSC Portrait Collection: Stacey's Book | $3.50 |
| ❑ MG92713-2 | | The Complete Guide to The Baby-sitters Club | $4.95 |
| ❑ MG47151-1 | | The Baby-sitters Club Chain Letter | $14.95 |
| ❑ MG48295-5 | | The Baby-sitters Club Secret Santa | $14.95 |
| ❑ MG45074-3 | | The Baby-sitters Club Notebook | $2.50 |
| ❑ MG44783-1 | | The Baby-sitters Club Postcard Book | $4.95 |

Available wherever you buy books...or use this order form.

- - - - - - - - - - - - - - - - - - - - - - - - - - - - - - - - - - - - - - - - - - - - - - - - - - - - - - - - -

**Scholastic Inc., P.O. Box 7502, 2931 E. McCarty Street, Jefferson City, MO 65102**

Please send me the books I have checked above. I am enclosing $_____
(please add $2.00 to cover shipping and handling). Send check or money order–
no cash or C.O.D.s please.

Name_____Birthdate_____

Address _____

City_____ State/Zip _____

# THE BABY-SITTERS CLUB

### by Ann M. Martin

## Collect and read these exciting BSC Super Specials, Mysteries, and Super Mysteries along with your favorite Baby-sitters Club books!

### BSC Super Specials

| | | |
|---|---|---|
| ❏ BBK44240-6 | Baby-sitters on Board! Super Special #1 | $3.95 |
| ❏ BBK44239-2 | Baby-sitters' Summer Vacation  Super Special #2 | $3.95 |
| ❏ BBK43973-1 | Baby-sitters' Winter Vacation  Super Special #3 | $3.95 |
| ❏ BBK42493-9 | Baby-sitters' Island Adventure  Super Special #4 | $3.95 |
| ❏ BBK43575-2 | California Girls!  Super Special #5 | $3.95 |
| ❏ BBK43576-0 | New York, New York!  Super Special #6 | $4.50 |
| ❏ BBK44963-X | Snowbound!  Super Special #7 | $3.95 |
| ❏ BBK44962-X | Baby-sitters at Shadow Lake  Super Special #8 | $3.95 |
| ❏ BBK45661-X | Starring The Baby-sitters Club!  Super Special #9 | $3.95 |
| ❏ BBK45674-1 | Sea City, Here We Come!  Super Special #10 | $3.95 |
| ❏ BBK47015-9 | The Baby-sitters Remember  Super Special #11 | $3.95 |
| ❏ BBK48308-0 | Here Come the Bridesmaids!  Super Special #12 | $3.95 |
| ❏ BBK22883-8 | Aloha, Baby-sitters!  Super Special #13 | $4.50 |
| ❏ BBK69126-X | BSC in the USA  Super Special #14 | $4.50 |
| ❏ BBK06000-7 | Baby-sitters' European Vacation  Super Special #15 | $4.50 |

### BSC Mysteries

| | | |
|---|---|---|
| ❏ BAI44084-5 | #1 Stacey and the Missing Ring | $3.50 |
| ❏ BAI44085-3 | #2 Beware Dawn! | $3.50 |
| ❏ BAI44799-8 | #3 Mallory and the Ghost Cat | $3.50 |
| ❏ BAI44800-5 | #4 Kristy and the Missing Child | $3.50 |
| ❏ BAI44801-3 | #5 Mary Anne and the Secret in the Attic | $3.50 |
| ❏ BAI44961-3 | #6 The Mystery at Claudia's House | $3.50 |
| ❏ BAI44960-5 | #7 Dawn and the Disappearing Dogs | $3.50 |
| ❏ BAI44959-1 | #8 Jessi and the Jewel Thieves | $3.50 |
| ❏ BAI44958-3 | #9 Kristy and the Haunted Mansion | $3.50 |
| ❏ BAI45696-2 | #10 Stacey and the Mystery Money | $3.50 |
| ❏ BAI47049-3 | #11 Claudia and the Mystery at the Museum | $3.50 |

**More titles ➡**

## The Baby-sitters Club books continued...

## Available wherever you buy books...or use this order form.

**Scholastic Inc., P.O. Box 7502, 2931 East McCarty Street, Jefferson City, MO 65102-7502**

Please send me the books I have checked above. I am enclosing $ _____
(please add $2.00 to cover shipping and handling). Send check or money order
— no cash or C.O.D.s please.

Name_____Birthdate_____

Address _____

City_____State/Zip_____

# THE BABY-SITTERS CLUB®

*Join Your BSC Friends on*

**CD-ROM!**

in

## 3rd Grade Learning Adventures
and
## 4th Grade Learning Adventures

Now **YOU** can join your BSC friends in a learning adventure featuring educational games and fun activities based on the experiences of the BSC!

## Each title features:

- •Over 40 exciting games, activities and subject areas
- •Interactive video of real-life BSC members
- •Many printable activities for hours of away-from-the-computer fun
- •Connection to BSC on-line community
- •Three skill levels
- •Builds 3rd and 4th grade skills in Math, Language Arts, Science and Social Studies
- •Windows 98/95 and Macintosh compatible

**Look for Baby-Sitters Club Learning Adventures wherever quality software is sold, or call 1-800-KID-XPRT to order by phone!**

BSCD898